Swallows]
Autu.....

Sebastian Swan

Dedicated to all the nowhere people.

He is a real nowhere man,
Living in a nowhere land,
Writing all his nowhere thoughts,
For nobody.

(John Winston Lennon)

I chose the name *Tom* in memory of my cousin who died recently.

I remember too, my friend Stuart, and his kindness over the years.

All rights reserved.

No part of this publication may be reproduced or transmitted, in any form or by any means, without prior permission from the author.

Copyright: David Mattches, 2013

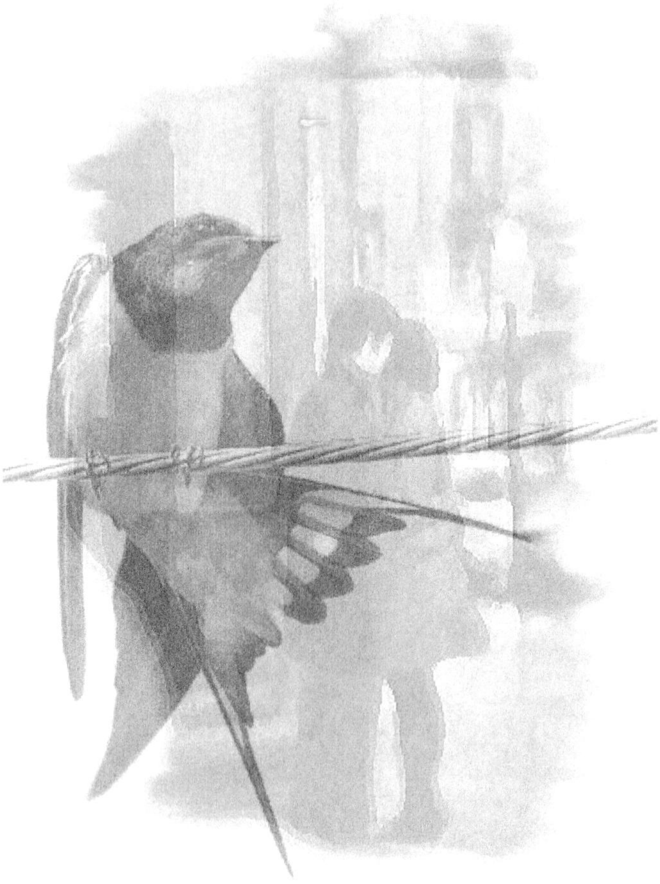

Thanks to:

Bob Watson for all the help he has given to me. Bob – has taught me everything I know about writing, he is simply the best. He is the only person I know who ISN'T – an expert.

Carolyn, for all her enduring support and kindness, she is truly an extraordinary person. (Friendship)

Doctor Miller for, her help, and advice.

Many of the places mentioned in this book are real, but all the people are fictitious any similarities are purely coincidental. All thoughts or comments and opinions are from the author's own imagination and should not be attributed to any third party. Historical information has on occasion been adjusted to fit the story.

Thanks to June for all her suffering for the sake of literature

The cover artwork is by the author.
If the reader has any comments about the book, the author would be pleased to hear from you.

sebastian.dave.swan@gmail.com

Follow *Sebastian Swan* on "Face Book".

Sebastian Swan was born in the North East of England not far from Bamburgh, he lectured in Yorkshire, then as the salmon returns to the place of its birth, he returned to the North East when he retired, and started to write. All his life he had struggled with the written word, being dyslexic. Where he did excel was his artwork, he drew and painted from being a small boy.

He had cancer, which forced him to retire, while he was ill he started to read for pleasure, he couldn't do much else for a while. He found that in reading he could be transported to another place, a "Dream World". One day he thought he could create his own dream world and started to write, with a little help from his friends, and drew from the vast resources of history and beauty on his doorstep. Most of his books are played out in the beautiful North East of England, where the places in the books can be seen and touched.

Come to the North East, sit on the quiet beaches, close your eyes, and be transported into the world of Sebastian Swan.

David Mattches BA

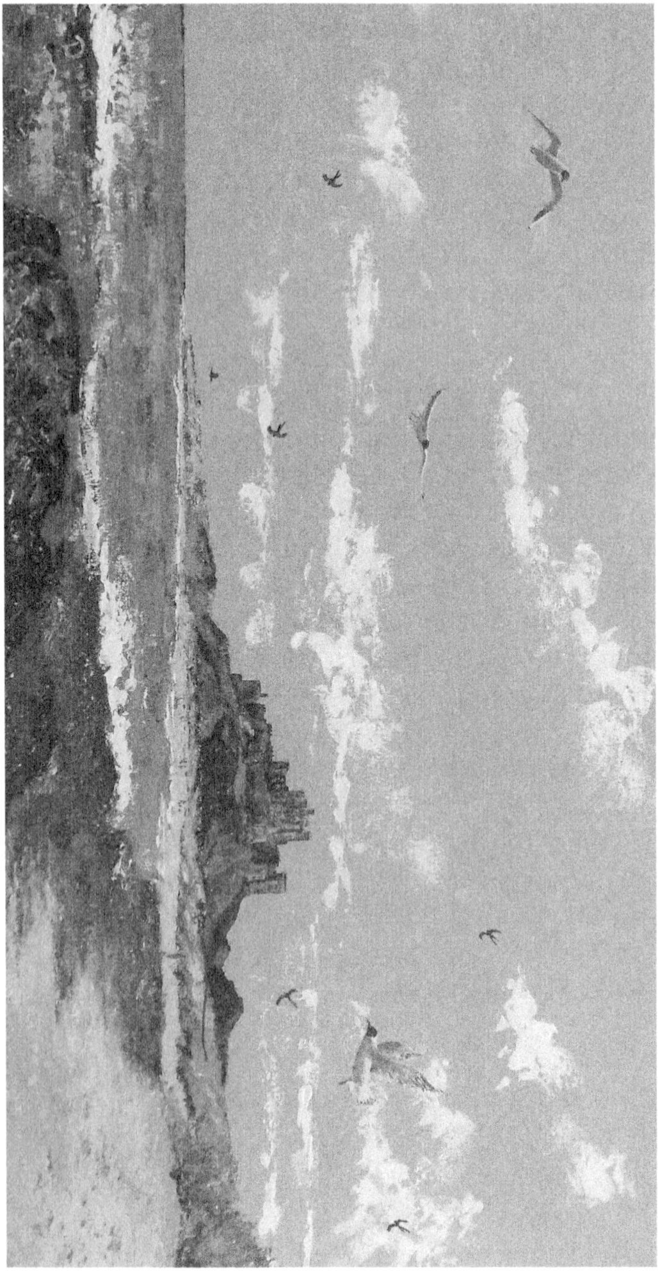

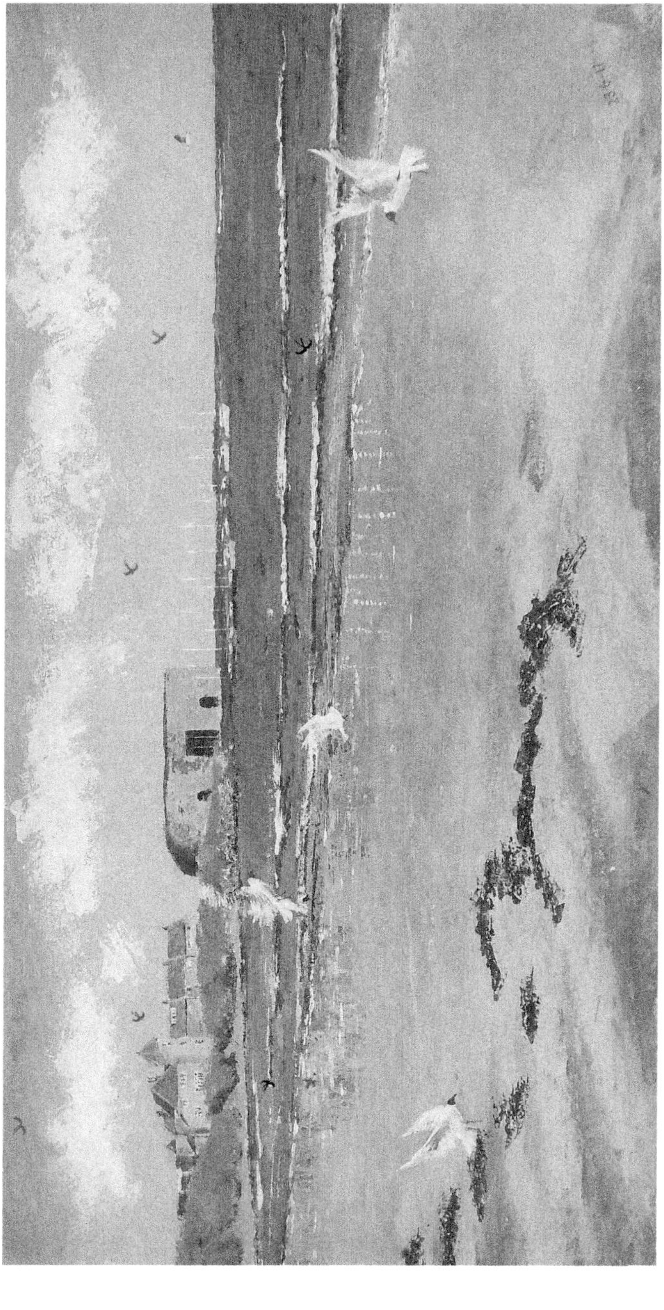

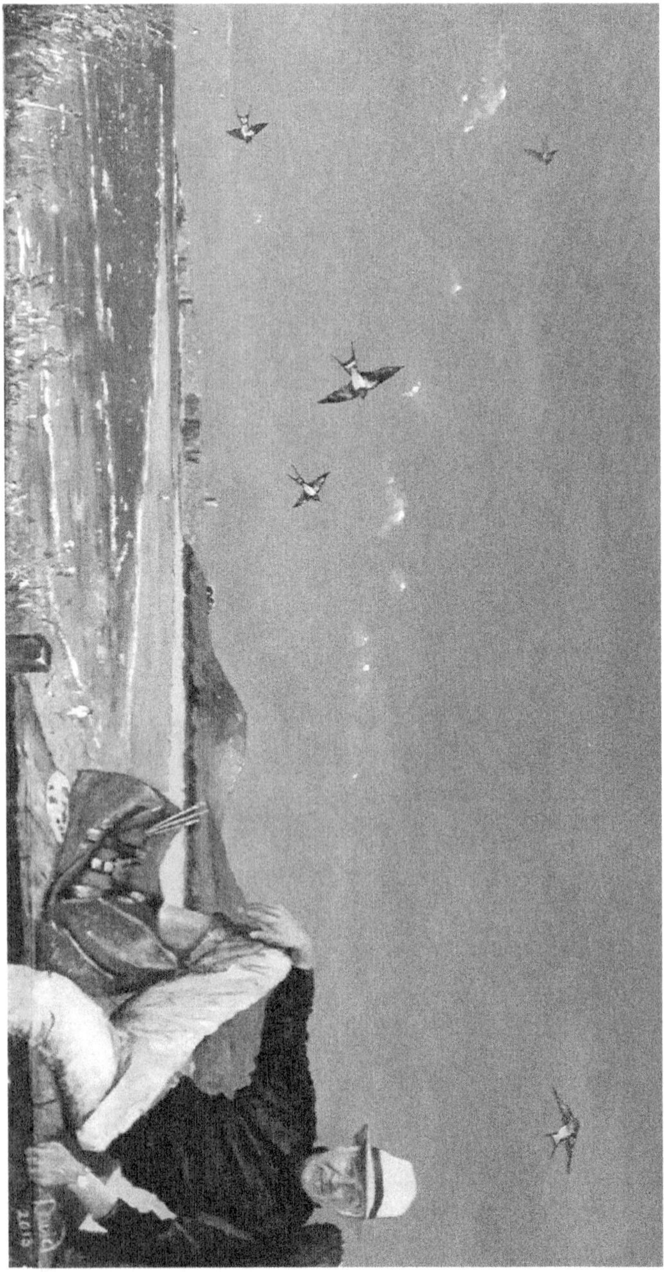

Geordie Dictionary

For those amongst my readers who are not familiar with God's own language, below are some helpful translations.

Bairn:	Child
Bloke:	Man
Bonny lad:	A greeting to a friend or child
Caad:	Cold
Comfy:	Comfortable
Dee:	Do
Diven't a nah ye:	Don't I know you
Frock:	A dress
Gannin:	Going
Howay:	Come on
Hinny:	Term of endearment
Hoose:	House
Hoy:	This is a way of attracting attention
Knaa:	Know
Lang:	Long
Lass:	Often used when referring to one's wife or girl friend
Muckle:	Big or large
Nivvor:	Never
Nowt:	Nothing
Oot:	Out
Pet:	A term of endearment such a honey or darling
Siven:	Seven
Tee:	To
Toon:	Town, in particular Newcastle

Whey-man:	A term of disbelief, "Well I never"
Whey-aye:	Of course
Wor:	Our
Yasel:	Yourself
Ye're/Ya're:	You are
Yee:	You

Chapter One

The "Fisherman's Rest" was packed right to the outside door. Wriggling, squeezing, and apologising his way to the exit, Tom eventually pushed the door open and literally tumbled outside.

'Phewww, it was flipping hot in there, I need some fresh air,' he said to himself taking a deep breath. While he had struggled his way through the hot sweaty throng, someone must have accidentally poured beer down his back, now that he could actually lift his arm above his waist, he felt his shirt, and it was saturated.

Once a month there was a folk-night, and everybody and his dog came, prepared to offer their unique contribution. It was a happy good natured evening, but tonight it was the busiest he had seen the place, standing room only, no one could get to the bar for a drink, that's if you could see the bar through the dense cloud of cigarette smoke. Drinks were passed back over people's heads with much of the contents of the glass being spilt on its journey. The noise was deafening, what with the music and people shouting to be heard, any hope of conversation was impossible. He even wondered at one point, if they were actually playing the same tune, but it didn't seem to matter, either way, everyone appeared to be enjoying the mayhem. There wasn't room to swing a kitten never mind a cat.

Tom had lived here for six months, it was a friendly little fishing village no more than a couple of dozen whitewashed houses nestled by the shore; he loved the place.

From the house he had rented, he could see beyond the bay to the ruined castle, a relic from the Wars of the Roses he reckoned. His home was very basic, it didn't even have a flush toilet, the toilet was situated, "Out the back", and the arrangement he doubted had changed much since man first settled there.

The only hot water he had was what he heated on his Victorian cast-iron range. He mainly cooked on a Calor gas stove, but it was a dirty business, it seemed to make everything sooty, he wondered if it was set-up correctly.

He had three rooms, a kitchen, (No hot water) a bedroom, and one with two old leather armchairs, where he ate his meals. The floors were covered with wood patterned linoleum, with a couple of, what his mother called, "Clippie mats" one in his bedroom and one in front of the fire in the main room. They were made from bits of old clothing cut up into strips. He could remember helping her draw out the designs on sheets of paper, then she would stretch a hessian backing over a wooden frame and weave in the pieces of cloth with a tool called a bodger. His mother had told him that mats like this were made by Vikings; she had once seen some pieces in a museum. He thought that they were beautiful like pictures in cloth.

Tom was sure that those days were passing into history. As far as he could tell, people, in general, seem to be a lot better off. They had had enough of austerity over the war years, and they wanted "New", and they didn't want to wait. Ordinary people now had money left over at the end of the week, and that would be spent on luxuries and leisure, as the Conservative Prime Minister, Harold Macmillan said, "You've never had it so good". I don't know that we are any happier, Tom thought. Of the other two rooms, one Tom slept in, the other he used for his studio, and it was piled high with canvases for his forthcoming exhibition in Newcastle, at least that was the plan. The whole place stank of oil paint.

Tom had been an art teacher, he had a degree in art, but he never took to teaching, he had given it a whirl for three years, but the kids "Had his life", as he put it. He knew he was a hopeless teacher; the "Little beasts" spent most of his lessons flicking paint at each other. As soon as the bell went, they shot out of the classroom, when the dust settled the classroom looked as if a bomb had hit it, a very colourful bomb, it had to be said.

He decided to leave before he was asked to. When he offered his resignation to the Head, the Head looked equally relieved, saying, "Well, Mr Jackson, teaching is not for everyone".

No falling on his knees begging him to stay, Tom felt a little hurt. He had tried; a modest flicker of remorse that he was leaving would not have cost the Head much, but no. Perhaps the Head was frightened he might change his mind, "Ha, fat chance, I will beg on the streets before I darken these doors again", he thought. Tom walked out of the yard, caught the number 32 bus home, and never looked back. He didn't know what the future held, BUT! It would not include snotty nosed kids who thought rococo was some sort of chocolate drink and *Monet* was what Frenchmen spent. That was what he told one of his colleagues, who looked at him in horror, when she asked with genuine concern, "How are you going to manage?" Tom was compelled to smile as he recalled the moment. The poor woman had taught all her life, like her father before her, and really didn't know what the rest of the world could possibly be doing every day. Going to school was an end in itself for her; it was all she had known since she was five years old. When she said someone was exceptionally bright, she meant that they had passed lots of exams and ideally, they had become teachers, and so they repeated the cycle, all very neat.

Tom was going to be the exception to the rule if this was all life had to offer; jumping off the Tyne Bridge was singularly more attractive. Mark Twain hit the nail on the head as far as Tom was concerned, when he said, "You should never let schooling interfere with your education".

Tom had no family to speak of, in the sense of uncles, aunts and cousins, just his two brothers, Fred and Michael and a sister, Molly. His brothers both worked as welders at Johnston and Short's shipyard. Molly had worked in the office at Shorts as a typist where she'd met Jim Keble, who she'd married. Tom thought Jim was a decent enough bloke. He worked as a draughtsman, a white-collar job, and was good at it by all accounts, he must have been, and he'd recently been promoted to supervisor. Molly and Jim were even buying their own house. Michael was married to Jean Walker, who worked on the tobacco counter at the new supermarket. Fred, the eldest, was married to Maureen Wilson who'd worked with Jean, and they had a two-year-old daughter Peggy.

Of all his siblings, he got on best with his sister Molly, but really, he never felt to have much in common with any of them.

Both his mum and dad were only ones, and his grandparents were dead.

He only ever knew his maternal grandfather and grandmother, and they were tragically killed in a house fire when Tom was ten, he remembered it vividly. His granddad had dementia, and it was suspected that he had started the fire, but nothing was ever proven.

That was an awful time; his mother was in a terrible state, day after day she cried. Unfortunately, his father was unable to give her the love and tenderness she needed. Tom thought that in some way it bonded him and his mother even closer together because he was the one who was able to show her the concern and affection she needed. Even his sister didn't seem to be able to reach his mum, but then she was ever her dad's girl. His father had always been able to cuddle Molly; in his eyes, she could do no wrong.

It wasn't that his father didn't love his mother, he was sure he did, but he was not capable of showing obvious affection. Tom could not remember his father ever saying to his mother that he loved her, and he never saw him kiss her. His father had died in an accident in the shipyard. Tom didn't really miss him, they were never close, his father thought that art was for "Puffs and dagos" as he put it, and no son of his was going to be involved with, "Owt Like that". He was very close to his mother; he took after her in nature and looks. He was tall with thick black hair and sparkling blue eyes, like her.

She always encouraged him, she liked to draw too, but she had no time, not with four kids to bring up, she never stopped working. "Flipping heck she had it hard", he often thought since and regretted that he had not done more to help her. While he was "Dossing" at university making models from beer cans (empty beer cans) and calling it conceptual art, she was working her, "Fingers to the bone".

Once his dad died, she took in washing and cleaned at the local school, so he could go to the grammar school and then to university. When he looked back, he was filled with remorse. He couldn't remember his mother; ever buying a new dress, or new shoes, they were always second-hand. She never treated herself. She had been a beautiful woman, with thick black wavy hair. He remembered her when he was small, she was striking, but once his father died, she had cut her hair short, and never went to the hairdressers, "Hairdresser's costs money", was her constant answer if ever he mentioned it.

The summer he finished at university, he had gone in to see her in her bedroom, taking her a cup of tea, wondering why she wasn't up. She had looked worn out when she went up to bed the night before. He stared at her, she appeared as if she was sleeping, but she was dead, he couldn't believe it. Somehow, in his pathetic innocence he thought she would be there forever, he supposed most kids thought the same. He couldn't even contribute towards the funeral cost, which was down to his brothers, sister, and brother-in-law. He had taken it all and given nothing. They never said anything to him, which made him feel even more wretched. He was our Tom, the bright one, and the university graduate, too important to contribute to his mother's funeral, you couldn't expect him to he was educated.

All pathetic thought Tom, what a dead loss, so much for education, you pass a few exams, and that entitles you to take advantage of everyone. He felt all education had done for him was to show him what a parasite he was.

Tom felt that he was always the odd one out, his mother's favourite, perhaps because he was the baby of the family.

Whatever the reason, they were close, and he loved her dearly. It was almost as if his mother had just clung on to life long enough to see him "Fixed up", as she put it. He knew how proud she was of him, none of the mothers up the street could boast of a son with a degree.

He had once sworn at her, to his everlasting shame, because she had embarrassed him in front of a neighbour when he passed his A-Levels. He couldn't even let her have her pride as a reward for all her relentless self-sacrifice. Yes, he had loved her, but he didn't know how much until she died. Isn't that ever the case, he had often thought since 'I'd give anything just to have another five minutes with her.' He swore then that he would never again take someone's love for granted. That seemed to be his regular prayer, whenever he went to put some flowers on her grave.

Was that all there was? Work and more work then you died.

Tom had continued to live in his mother's house once he started teaching at the local secondary school, but that was all in the past. He was now going to pursue a new career, his first love – painting. He had rented a small cottage in a little fishing village on the Northumberland coast, and he intended to see if he could make enough to survive. He had saved up some money while he had been teaching and that would keep him for a while until he had enough work for an exhibition.

He wasn't under any illusion, he knew that the graveyards were full of potential artists who had followed this path and died in obscurity. The odds were stacked against him, but he felt he must give the one talent he had, a fair chance. People told him he was very talented, his lecturers at the university had said he was *exceptional*, well he would see if *"exceptional"* sold pictures. Tom knew Vincent van Gogh, whose work he loved, was today proclaimed "One better than", *exceptional*, he was heralded as a genius, but he only sold one painting in his lifetime.

Poor Vincent, he had even eaten his paints and drunk turpentine, 'I'll settle for exceptional, the food might be more palatable,' he said to himself, smiling.

Tom was now closing the door of the only home he had ever known, for the final time, he had to tug it to close it; it had never closed properly as long as he could remember. He pushed the key through the letterbox of the house he'd lived in for twenty-five years. He kicked the door, rested his head against it for a few moments, turned, and walked off.

Chapter Two

Tom twisted his head from side to side shaking his shoulders, trying to rid himself of the crushed up feeling, he was glad to be out of the pub and in the fresh air. It was a beautiful warm sunny evening; the sea was as flat as a pancake.

He walked to a bench, which looked out to sea and seated himself down, linked his hands behind his head, stretched out his legs and breathed out the sigh of a man content with life. As he gazed along the beach past the blue and white fishing cobles, he caught sight of a lone walker in the distance coming towards him. The figure was no more than a couple of inches high, perhaps half a mile away. He didn't know it then, but this was the rest of his life walking towards him.

He stared at the figure, and he saw it was a young bare-footed woman wearing a short-sleeved white dress. As she drew closer, he saw, what he'd thought was a white dress, was, in fact, more like a loose shirt over a bathing costume. In her hand, she was clasping a white sun-hat. He'd never seen her before, must be a holidaymaker he thought. She came up the steps towards him, 'You've stolen my seat,' she said smiling.

'Room for two, I'll budge up.' She had one of those faces that smiled if one was fortunate enough to be caught in its warmth you could do no other than smile too. She flopped down beside him, stretching out her legs and fanned herself with her hat.

'Phew it's hot, what a glorious evening, I've just walked to the castle and back and I've never seen a soul, how wonderful.'

'You've been taking pictures.' He pointed to the camera around her neck.

'Some, not many, I was far too engaged in the magic of the place.'

'You on holiday?'

'Yes, I have taken a cottage up there for the summer,' she said pointing to a row of three white cottages halfway up the hill, 'and you, are you an invader too?'

'Actually... yes, *and* no, I am not a local born and bred, but I live here, for the moment anyway. I live up there,' he said pointing to the same three houses as her.

'Oh! So we are neighbours then?'

'Seems so, I'm Tom Jackson,' he said offering his hand.

'Pleased to meet you, I'm Jennifer Dunwoody, I live at number two.'

'I live at number four before you ask, I don't know how there can be a number four when there are only three of us.'

She laughed, 'Isn't that what's so perfect about this place, a mystery under every stone. I would love to live at number three, how neat to live at a house that's not there, it's sort of eternal. Perhaps that's where heaven is, at number three.' They both laughed.

'When you find it, let me know. You look hot, can I treat you to a drink, to show you how friendly the neighbours are here?'

'Ten out of ten for observation, dying of thirst *must* be written on my forehead? I just dumped my stuff when I arrived and went straight out for a walk on the beach.'

'It's a warm evening, and that's a fair walk, I thought you might be thirsty.'

'I certainly am, it sounded a bit hectic in there. I heard all the noise when I set off.'

'It was, that's why I came and sat here, but quite a few have left since I came out so we may be able to get a drink now if you fancy giving it a go?'

'Perfect, I have no money with me, I will pay you later.'

'Ah, no worries, my treat.' He followed her along the narrow path to the pub, she was thin, maybe too thin, but a good figure nevertheless, she was tall perhaps five eight he guessed, her hair was short sandy coloured. That's who she reminds me of – Audrey Hepburn, he thought. He felt his stomach; perhaps she wasn't so much thin, it was rather he, who was too fat. He had noticed that there was some surplus flesh at his waist, which was a new arrival. This sitting about painting was taking its toll, plus a staple diet of fish and chips. He just didn't have time to shop and cook, but he knew he needed to make some effort, and he made a firm resolution as they walked, to take more exercise.

'Gosh, it's hot in here,' she said, as she opened the door and the heat and the smoke billowed out.

'Not as bad as it was when I left. Look I can even see the bar now. What can I get you?'

'This is kind of you, may I have a pint of bitter shandy please?'

'Look *they're* leaving!' he said pointing to a table in the corner, 'Quick you grab those chairs, and I'll bring the drinks.' He paid the barmaid and picked up the two pint glasses, turning he saw Jennifer was already chatting to the people on the next table as if she had known them all her life, perhaps she had. Tom set the drink down on the table before her.

'Cheers, just what the doctor ordered,' she said reaching for it and took a long drink. 'I'm sorry, was it, Tom? I'm shocking with names.'

'Spot on, do you know those people?' he nodded towards the next table.

'Nope, I chat to everybody,' she took another drink from her glass and set it down on the table.

'Here,' Tom passed his handkerchief to her, 'the froth has left you with a bushy moustache, don't worry it's clean, the handkerchief I mean.'

She smiled, 'Thanks Tom, bet you've forgotten my name.'

'Now how likely am I to forget the name of a beautiful young woman?'

'Flatterer, so what is it?'

'Errr... was it Bob?' She laughed.

'Right in one.'

'So what do you do in this metropolis, Phil?' She teased, he laughed.

'Well, Bob, I'm a painter, of sorts and I came here to knock up some work for an exhibition.'

'How exciting, makes my life seem frightfully boring.'

'Why, what do you do?'

'I am a photographer for a local rag, but I'm having a break for a while, I have had a bit of an opp,' and now I'm doing a spot of convalescing.'

'Nothing serious I hope.'

'They say it all went well, now I need to rest and recover.'

'Like doing a four-mile hike sort of rest?'

'Ah, what does it matter, I will lie in bed tomorrow.'

They chatted and laughed, the talk was easy like old friends, she drained her glass, and Tom asked if she wanted another.

'No thanks, I'm as full as an egg, I must go and unpack before bedtime, as soon as I've done that I will get some fish and chips for my supper, I'm ever so hungry.'

'Tell you what, if you like *I* could get the fish, and chips while you unpack and you could join me, it would be a change, I usually eat alone.'

'You're on, I love the "Fish and chips" here. The fish is so fresh. We have come, that's my parents and I, to the northeast coast for holidays for as long as I can remember. I could eat the fish every day.'

'Now there's a thing, I actually do,' Tom said placing his hand on his stomach, they both laughed, 'I'll give you a shout when they are on the table. Come on, let's go.' It was still a bit of a squeeze to get to the door, and they were pressed together, for some unknown reason she reached up and kissed his cheek, she looked as surprised as he did.

'Now why on earth did I do that, I'm so sorry.'

'Hey I'm not complaining, it must be the beer and fresh air, gone to your head, I've never been kissed by a Bob before.'

'Anyway, I am sorry, perhaps it's just that you've made me feel happy, it seems a while since I laughed so much.'

'Come on, you need food.'

Just as they stepped out of the pub a young man, wearing a blazer and yellow paisley patterned cravat, walked towards them smiling at Jennifer.

'Jennifer, how jolly amazing bumping into you here, are you on holiday too?' He took her in his arms and kissed her on the lips, 'Come on darling, I'll buy you a drink.' He totally ignored Tom.

'I'll be off Jennifer,' Tom said feeling awkward and walking away, 'perhaps I'll see you around,' he called back over his shoulder.

'Who's that, one of the local yokels?' Tom heard the man say as he went, 'They are so tedious, don't you find.'

'Really Jeremy, how rude, that is my friend, and he is a gentleman, which you are not, I must go, I have a dinner appointment.' With that, she shrugged free of his arms and ran after Tom, leaving the young man with a look of utter disbelief.

'I'm so sorry about that Tom,' Jennifer said, when she caught up to him, 'what a ghastly man. His father is a friend of my father's, and Jeremy thinks he's God's gift to women, you must think me awfully rude, but I can't abide him. I hope the dinner invitation's still open?'

'Sure, I thought I was going to have to eat alone,' Tom smiled at her, 'but your friend was right you know, I'm more a yokel than a gentleman.'

'You heard him? Oh, I'm so sorry. I could kill him. Next, to that fellow, you are a gentleman believe me. He's a creep, always touching me as if... awe, let's forget about him, I hope he's not staying around here. Are you up for protecting a damsel in distress?'

'Just call me Sir Lancelot,' they both smiled at each other, holding eye contact a little longer than the moment called for.

As they neared the three cottages where Tom lived and the holiday cottage Jennifer was renting, Tom's eye lighted on the soft-top car stood on the road in front of number two.

'Wow, is that your flashy blue machine?'

'Yes, but it's not, *so* flashy.'

'It is, if you come from Waterloo Terrace, believe me. If it had been parked up our street, it would be standing on bricks by now without its wheels.' He smiled at her. She was quite startled by his smile. *Gosh, he is stunningly handsome* she thought, *and what's even more attractive is, that he behaves as if he is entirely oblivious to his good looks. Unlike that jerk, I have just bumped into.*

'Boy, photographers must get better wage packets than school teachers that's for sure,' Tom joked.

'Oh,' Jennifer said, concentrating once more, on what Tom was saying, 'I'm just lucky, that's me, lucky old Jennifer.'

'You make good fortune sound a heavy load, what sort is it, it's new to me,' Tom asked as he drew near and walked around it admiring the lines. 'I can't even drive.'

'It's a Triumph Vitesse, they are new.'

'Thought I'd never seen one before, but when you don't drive you tend not to pay much attention to cars. I'm jealous, perhaps I should have been a photographer.'

'Swap places.'

'Ah, I would probably crash it on the first outing. Why don't you unpack and I'll give you a shout when supper is served, how's that sound?'

'Cheers, sounds perfect. Give me half an hour to empty my case and hang up my things, and I'll be ready.'

'Half an hour it is then.' She left Tom and he went into his house to set the table. He set it with all the refinement he could manage considering the limited resources at hand, stood back and with a flash of inspiration, he decided to cut some dog roses from the hedge at the back of the house. He found a pair of scissors, went outside, and cut half a dozen of the best, tearing a chunk out of his wrist for the privilege. He sucked the wound and dabbed it with his handkerchief on his way back to the house. He arranged them in a vase, which he found under the sink. 'Hmm,' he said to himself, nodding in satisfaction at his artistic flair.

It was only a five-minute walk to the chip shop, by the time he returned the half hour was up and he knocked on Jennifer's door, opened it slightly and called in, 'Ready?'

'Yes, perfect timing,' he heard her respond as she came to the door smiling.

'Oh heck, you've changed, and I'm still wearing a beer-soaked shirt.'

'Actually, I didn't think my bathing costume was appropriate for dinner.'

'Ah, fair point, but you make me look every inch the yokel your friend mentioned.'

'You're fine and please don't refer to *him* as my friend. He very definitely is no friend of mine.'

'Oh, I'm sorry, the light in here will be *my* friend, it's not the best perhaps you won't notice my shabby apparel.'

Tom pushed at the door trying not to swear. It always required a strong arm to open it, it gave a sudden squeak and sprung open, and he showed her in.

'Oh Tom, how sweet, thank you, the flowers are beautiful, and candles too.'

'It's nothing,' he shrugged, 'I do this every day.'

'Of course, you do,' and they both laughed. Tom had the plates warming in the sink; he'd poured some more hot water over them. He dried them and passed them to her.

'Oh dear, you've cut yourself.'

'Ah, it's nothing.'

'There you go, help yourself. There's some Mateus Rose, it seems very popular, I like the bottle shape, not much of a connoisseur of wines I'm afraid, and some bread and butter.'

'A veritable feast, what more could one ask for.' They sat and talked without pause, somehow they managed to eat as well. Tom was surprised how effortless their talk was, just as it had been in the pub. It was as if they had known each other all their lives. There were none of those awkward moments where conversation dries up, as so often is the case with new relationships, such as this. Not that he could really call this a new "Relationship", they had only known each other for a couple of hours, and probably the rest of her holiday would be spent sightseeing.

'Are these some of your pictures,' she gestured to two hung on the wall.

'Heavens no, they are ghastly, all I hate about painting. They were here when I moved in, all part of the furniture.'

'That's a relief; I was trying to think of something polite to say about them so as not to offend. Are you going to show me any of your work?'

'Err... yes, only not tonight, it's too dark. I would rather wait until there is some daylight, I always say you only get one chance to make a first impression, and, someone with a *flash new car* could possibly be a potential buyer. On the other hand, you may end up preferring these hanging here, who can tell.'

She laughed, 'I doubt that very much, but you never know, I will look forward to that then.'

'I do know, you make me quite nervous, it matters what you think. I'm not picking up the vibrations of an undercover art critic, come to check out the amazing young artist by the sea, I hope?'

'No, you can rest easy on that one. I'm no art critic, so you have no worries there, I like what I like, and that's as far as it goes.'

After the meal, Tom made coffee, and they sat in his two armchairs and chatted and laughed until the early hours.

'Jen, you don't mind me calling you Jen, do you?' She shook her head, 'have you seen the time, it's nearly ten past one, you'll be shattered, what with your drive here and that long walk?'

'I should be, but strangely I'm not, however, I will go, or I will not last out this holiday. Thank you again, for this out of the ordinary evening,' she said reaching out her hand to him.'

'That's how it goes, already our relationship's lost its sparkle, and we are down to shaking hands.' She laughed, and he showed her out. 'Shall I walk you home or can you manage?'

'I might *just* manage, goodnight Tom.'

Chapter Three

Tom awoke to sunlight bursting through his bedroom window, the beams of light sparkled against the dust particles floating in the air. He blinked, stretched, and rubbed his eyes, trying to bring his wristwatch into focus.

'Flipping heck! It's only 5:30am, and I'm wide awake, almost.' He yawned and stretched again slipping his legs over the edge of the bed. He sat for a moment, scratched his head, then stood and went to the sink, filled the kettle, plugged it in and started making a cup of tea.

'I'm glad I invested in this electric kettle, much quicker than boiling water on the gas ring.' It only took a couple of minutes before it boiled and he "Mashed the tea", poured himself a mug and crashed down into his armchair. 'What day is this?' he asked himself, glancing at the calendar by the door... he paused, 'Sunday of course, it was the folk evening last night, and I met my new neighbour. She's all right, can't think when I last had such a good night.' I've forgotten living on my own what it is to be with people, it's a need, deep down, we all have he thought, for a whole host of reasons, somehow being with people sets the boundaries for self-worth. I wonder if she's busy today, a bit much to expect she might want to spend time with me a second day, not two in a row, *well* yesterday wasn't really a day, it was only last night, all night actually and a bit of this morning, come to think of it. Hang on boy, you don't fancy her, he smiled to himself, perhaps I do, she's a bit of all right, she even laughs at my jokes. Come to think of it I have never been out with a woman since I was at Uni' and that joke of a job laughingly called teaching, didn't give me time to breathe never mind have a social life. I wonder if I should knock on her door, ahhh, she will have plans. Give over, you're just scared in case she turns you down, can't hack the rejection.

He smiled, 'She was rather nice though, in fact very, very nice,' he said to himself. Tom wrestled the pros and cons back and forth debating with his alter ego. 'It's a good job she isn't privy to the ramblings in my mind, or you wouldn't see her for dust,' he said to himself. 'I'll bite the bullet and ask her, what the heck.' He made up his mind, filled the bowl in the sink with the rest of the warm water in the kettle, washed, and shaved. He splashed on some "Brut" aftershave from its chic green bottle with its personal silver medallion, his sister had bought it for his birthday; the first time he had used it.

He went back into the bedroom, slipped on his shorts and a clean shirt and looked again at his wristwatch, 'Ahhh, never, it's only twenty past six, blooming heck, she is going to like me waking her up at this time, she said she was going to lie in this morning. 'Ahhh,' he moaned again, 'What am I going to do now until I can call around without being a pest?'

He looked again at his watch, 'heaven's above what can I do for three hours or so, might as well go for a dander, pass some time. You realise, Tom, you are behaving like a twerp,' he said to himself.

What a fantastic morning he thought as he closed his door as quietly as he could, trying not to wake the whole neighbourhood. As he looked down to the shore he could see the sun was breaking through the sea-fret, the tide must be on the ebb, he thought.

'Phew, it's going to be a scorcher today,' he said to himself.

As he approached the seat near the pub where he had met Jennifer last night, he couldn't believe his eyes, she was there, sitting looking out to sea. As he neared, she turned at the sound of his feet on the gravel, her face lit up; he tried to be casual as if this was a normal occurrence, " Mr Cool". 'You won't be able to see far through that fret, but it will clear soon enough.'

'Morning Tom, I didn't disturb you, did I?' She turned back to the view. 'Looking into the mist is looking into the unknown; your imagination can kick in, a bit like the future. Do you never worry about the future, Tom; I mean, what it holds for you? Are you ever anxious, worried that you won't be able to face what it sends your way?'

'I was worried about my future this morning, that I might disturb my new neighbour,' she smiled, or at least her lips did.

'I couldn't sleep, and the sunlight didn't help. I was going to "Knock you up", as it were and see if you had any plans for today, but I thought you might not be awfully pleased.'

Tom sat by her, 'I must be honest; I went through the same thought pattern, I didn't want to disturb you. Anyway, I thought that you were having a lie in this morning.'

'Wish I could. Life's too short to lie in bed, it could be over tomorrow, Tom.'

'I can't say it was my first thought this morning.'

'No, probably not, life is forever at our age, isn't it?'

'That's the one.'

'Thanks for last night Tom,' she said as she looked at him, her eyes were bright with tears, she turned quickly away.

'Hey, you all right,' he touched her shoulder.

'Yes, yes, this morning sun is bright,' and she withdrew a handkerchief from her sleeve and touched her eyes then reached into her handbag and slipped on some sunglasses.

'Gosh, that sun is bright,' she said repeating herself.

'Fab,' he responded, letting the moment, and any questions in his mind pass.

'You smell nice.'

'Really – thanks,' he said as casually as he could as if this was just his normal everyday smell, and not a bottle he'd opened for the first time this morning. His Dad would have had a seizure if he'd known any of his sons were wearing perfume. He was still able to "Put the fear of God up" Tom and his dad had been dead for eight years. Tom shivered at the thought. Poor Dad, men were men in his world, whatever that meant, and they had short hair. He had been in the navy in the Second World War and fought at the River Plate against the Graf Spee, he was immensely proud of that.

Tom knew personally every shell they'd fired. Actually, he loved the story when he was young. When the movie came out with Peter Finch and John Gregson, he told all his mates that his dad had been there and basked in the reflected glory, pity his dad hadn't been able to see it, he thought. That was his dad's world and he struggled with the new youth-driven culture. The hair was too long, skirts were too short, the music was too loud, and it all sounded the same. "Discipline, that's what they needed", he would often say.

'About last night, I'm sorry for being so forward. I don't know what I was thinking about, you must think me awfully brazen, I am not at all like that. I know I talk to everyone, but most of its silly nervous chatter, in fact, I'm quite shy, strangely enough.'

'I don't think what you have to say is silly chatter, up to now you have held the interest of a very introvert boring person. You like to chat, and I have nothing to say, sounds like the perfect combination.'

'Thank you, Tom, you are not in the least boring, in fact, you are very interesting. I can't tell you how much I enjoyed last night. For a start, I don't know another artist. Having the courage to step out of the norm makes you interesting, and out of the ordinary. Talking to you last night was so effortless and natural. Perhaps we have met in another life, AND! I'm still embarrassed about that silly kiss.'

'Think nothing of it, Jen, it's my animal attraction, it's just something I have to live with, happens all the time.' She laughed, 'You can laugh, it's only two days since the last time I was caught unaware and very passionate it was too. You saw her last night she's called Dolly, the landlord's dog. I can tell you which I prefer, she's a very wet kisser, and her breath's shocking.'

'I suppose you've either got it or you haven't,' she said and they both laughed. 'It is strange though, I do feel that I have known you before, I can't believe it's only a few hours since I met you, everything is just so unforced.'

'Have you had any breakfast?'

'Not yet, I haven't a great appetite, I must be honest.'

'How's about I make you breakfast, I am a wiz at cereal and toast.'

'Thank you, kind Sir, that would be perfect. Lead on Macduff.' Tom stood, offered her his hand, and pulled her up. She's as light as a feather he thought.

'You need some dumplings, my girl, there's not a hapeth of flesh on you,' he said.

'No, I have lost quite a bit of weight lately.'

'Something to do with your operation?'

'Yes, probably, but nothing a steady diet of fish and chips and sea air won't sort out.'

'Ha, I am living testimony to that.' Tom didn't let go of her hand when he pulled her up off the bench, and she didn't seem to object.

Gosh, I like this girl, he said to himself I really do. It wasn't far up to their cottages, and they held hands as they walked. He had to push the door again to open it, 'Flipping thing's tight, do you know I lived for twenty odd years in the house where I was born, and that door never shut properly either, story of my life, as soon as I put my hand to a door there's a problem. There we go, you make the tea, or do you prefer coffee? Whatever you fancy, it's all in that cupboard. What am I saying! Whatever you fancy probably isn't in my cupboard, but there *is* a bottle of milk in that bucket of cold water by the sink, I find it keeps longer. I'll sort the toast and cereal, only cornflakes. You see I wasn't expecting to wake up this morning and have breakfast with a lady.'

Jennifer laughed, 'That's fine, I've got the milk,' she said, taking the bottle out of the bucket, 'all mod cons, no expense spared I see. I have a fridge next door if you want to use it.'

'A FRIDGE! *Wow,* the 60's have arrived.'

'And a flush loo and a bath.'

'With the risk of repeating myself, *wow*, I definitely drew the short straw, and no mistake, you wouldn't want to know the toilet arrangements here, believe me, but the price was right, cheap.'

'I suspected that this may be a little... quaint, is that the word, by the look of the place from the outside.'

'Ah... that's an interesting point, I have noticed, if the sun is shining; it's picturesque and quaint, but it's blowing a gale from the Arctic and lashing with rain, it's a slum.'

Jennifer laughed. 'Yes, I must say I hadn't thought of it like that. Now you mention it some of those charming white rustic cottages, one sees abroad, may fall into the slum category, were it not for the beautiful blue sky and the unrelenting sunshine. By the way, if you fancy a bath you are more than welcome to use mine, no lock on the door, I'm afraid.'

'Hey, I don't even have a door; come to think of it I don't have a bathroom. My bath hangs on the wall in the kitchen, but people know it all brings out the genius in us artists. Living in a hovel is part of the deal.'

'Is that so?'

'Definitely not for this artist, with a capital "*D*", here, your toast's ready.' They ate and chatted, oblivious to the passage of time. 'I will be drawing my old age pension before I know it if I spend much more time with you. Have you any idea what time it is?'

'Let me guess, three pots of tea past breakfast time.'

'Too right, it's a quarter past twelve.'

'Oops, oh, I'm sorry Tom, I'm wasting your time. Have you things to do? I guess you have.'

'Actually, I wondered if you might fancy going over to Bamburgh? They are playing cricket there this afternoon, chances are we've missed the start of the match, but hey, don't let me take over your holiday, you will have plans.'

'Wellllll actually, I was going to ask you if you fancied going for a drive in my car after you admired it so much last night, but I didn't like to ask.'

'We are a right pair. I would love a ride in your flash car, what about the cricket at

Bamburgh then? The good thing is even if you don't like cricket, it's a great way to relax in the sun.'

'Sounds perfect, is it played on the green under the castle?'

'Yep, if we tire of sitting we can go for a walk on the beach behind the castle. I'll tell you what, I have some sausages in my larder, how do you fancy collecting some driftwood and having a barbecue, in the dunes?'

'Oh Tom, that sounds perfect, this is shaping up to be an unforgettable holiday. But *wait* a minute, I thought you were going to show me your work today?'

'Ah, too hot today, another day will do.'

'Ha, too dark last night too hot today, I didn't know art was so governed by such precise conditions.'

He laughed, 'I like to keep my public in suspense, come on, you'll have that delight to look forward too.'

Chapter Four

'Wow, this is a touch faster than the United bus, my hairstyle will be ruined,' Tom laughed, as they sped along the country lanes towards the coast in Jennifer's new car.

'Look at that view before us, is that fantastic, or is that fantastic, Jen?' Tom said as the came over the brow of the hill towards the coast.

'It's fantastic, no question,' Jennifer couldn't help herself laughing she felt so happy. What a beautiful day she thought.

They drove on down to the sea and along the road, which followed the shoreline to Bamburgh. It took them through the small fishing communities; in the distance, they saw the magnificent castle at Bamburgh, which dominated the skyline. They could also see beyond it to the smaller castle of Holy Island.

As they entered the ancient village of Bamburgh, Tom said, 'You can park up the village, and we'll walk back to the castle.'

There was a parking spot by the village green, Jennifer took out a tartan rug from the boot of her car, and they walked back to the cricket match, which was being played out in the shadow of the castle.

As they walked, Jennifer looked up at the magnificent structure, 'That castle is something else, Tom.'

'Pretty impressive, eh.' To the side of the pitch, there was some raised ground with a path running along the top. They laid the rug at the bottom of the embankment, which gave them a backrest. Tom had brought a Thermos flask of tea; he usually took it when he went out painting for the day. 'I'll grab a couple of ice creams from that van and we can relax.' He quickly purchased the ice creams and sat down beside her.

'This is England at its best Jen, the sound of leather striking willow on the village green, sunshine and ice-cream and good company.'

'I think you are a romantic, Tom.'

'You think so.'

'I think so.' They ate their iced delight and lay back in the sunshine, to watch the match. After a while, Tom felt Jennifer's head roll against his chest, and when he looked down, he realised she was fast asleep. He placed his arm around her, and she snuggled into him.

Tom merely looked at her sleeping face, 'Boy oh, boy, is this my lucky day, she is beautiful.'

Jennifer awoke, to find the arm of a sleeping companion around her. She raised herself onto her elbow as carefully as she could, trying not to wake him, and smiled down at him. However, her movement had been enough to disturbed Tom, and he opened his eyes. He collected himself with a slight shake of his head, blinked, and smiled. Reaching up, he tenderly slid his hand around her neck and pushed his fingers into her hair, raising himself onto his elbow he kissed her. She merely relaxed into the embrace.

Slowly they parted, and he gently pressed his cheek to hers, 'It's now my turn to apologise, for impulsive kissing,' he whispered.

'Don't apologise, I wanted you to kiss me,' and their lips met again.

Releasing her, he looked into her eyes and smiled, and asked, 'Who's winning, I wonder?'

Her eyes never left his, they were so close she could still feel the warmth of his lips, 'It's a draw, oh, you meant the cricket,' they both laughed, 'not a clue, and I'm afraid I don't care.'

They heard a voice nearby, 'Young folks today, they have no shame,' but the eyes of Jennifer and Tom were locked together, and they merely smiled, nothing could steal this moment from them.

'Come on let's go,' Tom said, 'we've outstayed our welcome, we'll make that barbecue.' With that Jen eased herself up and reached down with her hand to him, giving him a tug, 'Cheers, my bottom's gone numb.'

That Sunday was the model for the days to follow. The time was spent laughing, playing, and eating. They went to the Farne Islands on a boat trip. Jennifer was in her element; she shot off four rolls of film, taking pictures of the seabirds and grey seals. Whilst they walked and clambered over one of the small islands, Tom tripped and fell back into a rock pool. Jennifer was in fits of laughter, as she watched Tom flailing his arms, trying to regain his balance, attempting to avoid the unavoidable. There was an almighty SPLASH, and the manoeuvre was completed, with him sitting up to his waist, in cold water.

Once he collected himself and stood up; Jennifer said 'Ohhh, Tom, I'm so sorry, but...' and she burst out laughing again as he stood in the middle of the rock pool, and placed a length of seaweed on his head.

'An apology is less than convincing I have to say, when you are laughing your head off. Perhaps if you were wet too, it would engender a note of sincerity.'

'Don't you dare,' Jennifer suddenly looked nervous. Tom waded out of the pool, and he reached for her. She turned to run, but she was too slow, he grabbed her and scooped her into his arms, pretending to throw her into the pool.

Giggling and screaming she cried, 'NO, NO, really Tom, I'm sorry.'

'Really?'

'Yes, really, really.'

'Mmm, if you're truly repentant I'll spare you,' and he set her down. Once he had released her, she pushed him, he stumbled back into the pool, and she ran off laughing.

'Right, you're for it now,' he stepped out of the pool and ran after her. Jennifer giggled all the time she ran, once he caught her, she turned quickly, leapt into his arms, and kissed him. He set her down, but she still held him, looking into his eyes.

'Ah, Tom, I am so, happy, you are such an extraordinary man. An extraordinary man,' she was suddenly serious and reached up on her tiptoes to him, slowly pressing her lips to his. Their lips parted, and she said, 'I am really sorry Tom, gosh, you are drenched.'

'I should think I am, it's very wet that water.'

'Don't start me off again,' she smiled, 'here, take that wet jumper off and put mine on, I will be fine with my anorak,' and she took off her jumper and gave it to him.

'It's a touch tight,' he said in a high voice, 'but thanks.' He put his arm around her, and they walked back to where the boat was moored.

They went to all the sites in the following weeks, Holy Island, Alnwick, the Cheviot Hills, even the wet days were beautiful, they were just different types of beautiful day. Tom usually took painting materials with him, and Jennifer would take photographs of him, or she would quietly sit and watch him. She was frightened of her feelings. She knew this was all going to end, and it was going to end badly, that was the only option. Several times, she had to fight back the tears, to avoid questions; Tom was never going to understand this.

Chapter Five

They were both sitting on Tom's makeshift bench, which was merely a plank on two small beer crates. They sat with their legs stretched out leaning against the house wall, each with a mug of steaming hot coffee.

'Any chance of doing me a favour Jen?'

'If I can, depends what it is.'

'Would you sit for me?'

'You want to *paint* me!' She asked genuinely surprised. 'Who on earth would want a picture of me?'

'I would,' Tom said looking earnestly into his cup.

'Awe Tom, you are sweet,' she said kissing his cheek, 'Will it be, au naturel, I have heard about you artists?'

'Now there's a thought, I could sell tickets,' he looked up and smiled.

'Ha, more likely you would have to pay people to look at me naked.'

'Seriously, would you sit for me, actually, it was a portrait I had in mind?'

'If you want, but wouldn't it be a waste of your time, when you have work to do for your exhibition?'

'Not at all, it will be the centrepiece. Come on then let's get started now.'

'What, but I'm a mess.'

'No, you are perfect.' They drank up, and went inside to Tom's makeshift studio. He lifted one of his armchairs, which stood by the fire, into the position he wanted her to sit, and then he set up his easel.

'What do I do, do you want me to smile or what?'

'Just relax and be yourself, talk to me, if I wanted a photograph I would use a camera, I want a picture of you, a picture that captures what you are, the person I, lo... see.' She knew that he nearly said love and she was afraid. Suddenly, she realised for the first time, how could she be so blind... that was what she felt, she was in love with this man, how could she be so stupid. It was as if someone had switched a light on, oh God what a mess, she thought. She was serious now, he never seemed to notice, he was in another place his brush moved quickly it appeared to have a life of its own.

'Tell me Jen if you need a rest or want to stand up.' It was easy for her to keep still, her head was filled with thoughts, and she was relieved to be quiet. She would have to leave him. I don't know how I will do it, *if* I can do it, but this isn't fair on him, she thought as she sat, now feeling utterly miserable.

Tom, wouldn't let her see the work, his face was intense. She wasn't sure if it was the swirling in her head or the smell of the paint, but she felt quite light-headed.

'Phew, I need a rest, we'll have a break and some food, come on we'll go down to the pub, and see what they've got for lunch. They have started serving scampi in a basket, very trendy.'

'May I see what you have done before we go?'

'No! Not at this stage,' Tom said pulling a face, 'sorry.'

'That's jolly mean, of you Mr Jackson,' Jennifer said desperately trying to lighten her mood before Tom noticed.

'Not at all, to make up for it, I'll *treat you* to scampi and chips, how's that for a compromise? I'm sorry, but you'll have to suffer the pangs of curiosity until it's finished.'

'*Meanie*,' Tom laughed and hugged her. Jennifer tried to sneak a look as she passed the canvas, but he ushered her out. Actually, she was glad to be out in the fresh air and took some deep breaths to clear her head.

'I don't know how you stand the smell of that paint all day, Tom, it gets down my throat.'

'Sorry about that, I never thought, I'll open the back-door this afternoon, and we will have a through draught, that should help.'

Tom worked on the portrait for three days, there were coffee breaks of course, and in the evening, they would walk on the beach. Jennifer knew this was wrong, but he breathed life into her as surely as he was breathing life into her portrait.

They held hands now, wherever they went, it was merely how their relationship had developed, touching and holding each other was becoming a necessity, though they hadn't quite realised it yet. As they walked, Tom abruptly stopped and turned her to him, he laid his hand against her cheek and tenderly brushed a strand of hair from her face. He slowly lowered his lips to hers and she willingly responded, she couldn't help it, she didn't want to, it was unkind, she knew that, but she was not in control, there were other forces at work here. Their lips touched and pressed together, he took her in his arms and she held his head, preventing their lips from separating. She wanted him, her head was spinning, she couldn't think, don't let go of me Tom, she thought, I will fall. Gradually they released each other.

The spell was broken by two fishermen leaning against their boat, smoking. They clapped their hands, and called to them, laughing, 'Glad to see romance is not dead.' It was hard to tell who blushed the most, Tom or Jennifer. They looked towards the two fishermen, then they turned back to face each other and were compelled to laugh too.

'Now then Tom, if you could paint that picture I would buy it, young love, nothing like it, for warming the heart.'

'I'll see what I can do for you Jack, but you will have to wait, we're off for a drink in the pub.'

'Aye, we'll join you once we have straightened up here. I don't know what you sees in Tom's ugly mug, Jennifer, when there is handsome fellows the likes of me around.'

'If she was fifty years older and blind, you might be in with a chance, Jack,' his friend George said, and they all laughed.

It was on the fourth afternoon and finally, he was satisfied and stepped back twisting his head from one side to the other.

'Mmm,' was all he said.

'Can I see it?' Jennifer asked.

'If you must.'

'I feel a bit nervous,' she said rising from the chair and stepping towards him. She took his hand and then turned to the easel.

'Tom,' she gasped, 'is that how you see me? It's, I don't know what to say, I have never seen anything like it.'

'That good, eh.'

'Don't joke, Tom, to say it's beautiful doesn't describe it. It's alive, breathing, I feel as if I could talk to her, it's incredible. Truly, I have never seen anything like it in my life, it's the strangest thing, it's as if she wants to say something.' She wished she hadn't said that she knew what this image, this living image, was saying, "You have captured my heart, my soul, for all time, and I love you". That's what this girl was saying, she was afraid, and tears filled her eyes. It was all too much, this was killing her, 'I need to walk Tom, and walk, and walk.'

Chapter Six

The evening was humid, there was a storm brewing, Tom remarked looking up at the clouds. Jennifer looked up too, 'Mmm,' she said, it wasn't helping clear her head, she was sweating, her mind was a confused tangle. They went down to the water's edge hoping to find some relief from the humidity.

Slipping off their sandals and carrying them, they strolled slowly arm in arm, at the water's edge as it ran lazily up the golden sand.

Tom looked down at Jennifer's serious face, 'A penny for them,' Tom said.

'What!'

'You're very thoughtful, are you upset with the painting; it's just how *I* see you, or are you simply tired, it's tedious for you sitting all that time?'

'No, it's none of those things I told you, how could one possibly not like it? It's breathtaking. I feel humbled that you could see me like that. It's certainly not, how I see myself. She is beautiful, enigmatic. You have climbed into her soul. It's quite frightening as if you know me better than I know myself, it's just as I said, it's alive.'

'Give me a smile then.' He threw his sandals up the beach clear of the water and grabbed her by the waist turning her to him, and lifting her out of the water then he set her back down and tickled her. Her mood was abruptly transformed, and she giggled. She squirmed laughing and pushing herself away from him, arching her back. Tom drew her to him and pressed his lips to her extended throat. Gradually she stilled, lifting her head, her eyes sparkled as they met his. Jennifer lifted her arms, wrapping them around his neck and pulled herself up to his lips kissing him passionately. The kiss was heady but sweet and tender, she felt him move back on his heels to keep his balance, and she swayed against him, her voice was husky and laboured as she spoke. Looking into his eyes, she whispered, her lips still touching his, 'I can't say what I want to say,' she took his hand and placed it on her heart. 'Can you feel?'

'I can say what's on my heart, I...' She placed her finger on his lips.

'Don't say it, I don't want to hear it.'

'What! It makes the world go around, they say.'

'I don't want the world to go around I want it to stop, this minute. I want to hold this moment and this feeling forever. Please, time don't move on.' She turned away from him, and he released her, he was hurt and confused. He stood for a moment then placed his hands on her shoulders and turned her around to face him, tears were running down her cheeks.

'Hey, what's all this for, you'll scare all our swallows away, they've flown all the way from Africa just for us.' She held him and sobbed into his chest. He rested his cheek on her head, 'Come on Bob, nothing's that bad.'

'Tom,' she sobbed, 'you're a fool and I'm the cruelest person you've ever met, just go away and forget you ever saw me. I go tomorrow, that's the best for all.'

'I didn't know it was tomorrow you were going, you never said.'

'I have been putting off saying anything, hoping it would never come, this is the end for us, Tom.'

'You what! You are joking me; you mean never see each other again? You can't be serious.'

'Sorry Tom, it has to be this way.'

'Oh great, so you have decided what's the best for all.' Now he was hurt, confused, angry, he didn't know what. 'I just forget all about you, and get on with my work, like we never met, never laughed, never kissed, fantastic, is that it?' he pushed her away, she came back towards him, but he turned his palms towards her. The hands, which had held her moments since, now signified a barrier between them.

'Please Tom.'

'Please Tom, you are joking. Ohhh, I get it, stupid or what, you're married that's it, isn't it?'

'No, I'm not married.'

'You're engaged, or have a boyfriend you're two-timing.'

'None of those things, you don't understand.'

'You are flipping well right there. Anyway I know when it's time to go, never let it be said I don't know when I'm not wanted, drive safely.'

He turned leaving her sobbing, she called after him, 'TOM,' but he ignored her, he stooped to pick up his sandals and walked off. Unexpectedly there was a crash of thunder, and the heavens opened. Tom walked up the hill to his house, kicked the door open, as he entered he glanced once more to where he had left her, she was on her knees now, sobbing her heart out. The rain was coming down in sheets. She was wet through, 'Serves her right, her own stupid fault, she can drown for all I care.'

He slammed the door and kicked it shut, 'Bloody door.' He was soaking wet, what did it matter to him, he flopped down on his bed. He wanted to cry, he needed to cry, but the tears wouldn't come. He ran his fingers up over his face, squeezing his head between his hands gripping his hair and tugging his head from side to side, as he tried to bring some order to the turmoil within his brain, but he couldn't. He had never felt such confusion in his head before. His whole body was in torment. He wanted a drink, anything to deaden this agony, but he had no alcohol in the house. He lay on his bed curled up in the foetal position for most of the night. As the burgeoning daylight forced its way into the darkness of his hell, he could see out of the corner of his eye, a note sticking through the letterbox in the front door.

He nervously eased himself up, slid his legs over the edge of the bed, made his way over to the door, and pulled it free from the letterbox. He squeezed his eyes tightly closed, dreading to read what was written on the note. He clasped it in his hand for a minute, and then flicked the note with his thumb, and looked at it, all it said was, *"Goodbye, thank you, I'm sorry, x"*. He paused then frantically tugged open the door and looked towards number two, but she had gone. He turned to the whitewashed wall of his house and banged his head mercilessly against the wall; there was no pain, the blood ran down his face. He felt dizzy and collapsed onto his knees and knelt silently, he still held the note in his hand it was soaked with blood.

How long he had been knelt there, he didn't know. Eventually, he raised himself went inside his house and flopped down in his armchair. The pain had all gone now, he felt nothing, he had no sense of anything, sound, smell, feeling, he was dead.

He looked up at the half-closed front door it was dark outside, the floor was sodden from the rain, I must have been sitting here all day, he thought. Shaking his head he rose and went to close the door, he wanted to take one more look outside, but he knew it would be in vain, he forced the door shut and went back to his chair. He looked at the bloodstained note it was still in his clenched hand.

His eyes set on her portrait, she was smiling down at him, was she mocking him? No... that smile, that face never mocked, he couldn't see any deceit or unkindness in those eyes. 'If I paint for the rest of my life I will never better that picture, it is perfect, she was perfect, why, why, why?'

Chapter Seven

The days were pitifully miserable after she went. Tom had always enjoyed his own company; in fact, time on his own was essential to him to recharge his batteries, but he understood now that being on ones own was very definitely not the same as being *alone*.

There were times when he simply wanted to scream, such was the ache of the loneliness he was now experiencing. Most days he slipped away from the village and hid in the sand dunes and he would sit there all day. He couldn't even stand the occasional screech of a passing seagull.

He wanted and craved utter silence, it was in a sense, a sort of meditative condition, where he was trying to abandon his body and the pain and find a place of peace. He would leave his house before light and not return until dark, endeavouring to avoid contact with people. On one such occasion, he stayed out all night, staggering home exhausted in the early hours. He couldn't eat and hardly drank. He hadn't washed; his clothes were hanging on him. He was filthy now, and he'd grown a beard. After one such day out in the cold, he made his way unsteadily back to his house.

He was struggling to focus his eyes, feeling light headed and confused. When he eventually reached for the front door, his hand was trembling. He pushed the door open and went straight into the kitchen and filled a mug with water, his mouth was like dried parchment. His hand shook, his head began to spin and he dropped the mug, it shattered as it hit the stone sink. He stumbled back against the wall and slid down to the floor. Lifting his hands to his face he wept. These were the first tears since she had left.

When he had collected himself sufficiently to stand, he reached again to the shelf and took another mug, filled *it* with water and drank it, only cursorily glancing at the broken one in the sink. He filled it again, and sat at his easel, stared at it for some minutes then picked up a brush squeezed out some "Parasian Blue", white and "Briljant Yellow Light" onto his palette and started to paint. The tears continued he cuffed them away with his forearm.

As he painted the pain eased, this would be his, opium, his way to oblivion; he would paint, and paint. The next weeks he worked tirelessly, sometimes he merely slithered onto the floor when he was exhausted and slept where he fell. At times, he awoke still holding a paintbrush or a tube of paint in his hand.

He had no idea if the work was good or bad, what did it matter? He was painting from some place within, an expression of his humanity, never had he been so conscious of human frailties, and the fragile path life travelled. His brush strokes created swallows, swooping and diving, graceful blue flashes of light against the sky and the sea. He didn't seem to be in control, the brush movement was rapid and spontaneous, the canvas was given life, then it was replaced and the process began again.

Then the day came when he was finished, or was he simply worn out. He sat down in his armchair, his paintbrushes in one hand and palette in the other and stared at the pile of canvases. There was barely room to stretch out his legs, he was trembling he was so weak he felt ill.

He struggled out of his chair and went to the kitchen to see if he could find anything to eat. All he could find was some mouldy bread and half a packet of soggy cornflakes, he hadn't any milk, the milk in the bottle he had was alive and growing. So, he made the best of what he had, tipped some sugar over the cereal, and ate it. He ate two bowls full and then made some sweet black coffee, gradually he felt a little better. He sat for a while, trying to make some sense of his life, he had a blinding headache. He took the tin bath down from a hook on the kitchen wall, made room for it amongst the debris, boiled some water, filled it, and bathed. He dried himself on his shirt because he couldn't find a towel or was too weary to look for one. Everything he did, he did it slowly, he opened his eyes slowly, he turned slowly, and he thought slowly, living it seemed, required resources he no longer had.

Some how, he didn't know how, he made his way to Newcastle and organised an exhibition, and transport for his work and returned home. He had to make himself put one foot in front of the other. It seemed as if his future was going to have to be hewn out of rock. Every step was a battle of the will. He didn't know how long he would be able to live life like this. It was just too difficult, the effort required was more than he could sustain.

Tom didn't paint anymore when he returned home from Newcastle. It was as if what had been there was now on canvas. While he waited for his exhibition, he walked, back and forth along the miles of white sand. Neither wind nor rain made any difference; he knew then that any normal human feelings of cold, hunger, or physical pain were never to be his again.

Whenever he climbed up the incline from the beach past the bench where he and Jennifer had met, he turned away. He would never sit there again as long as he lived, he couldn't even bear to look at the place, he knew that he would live here for the rest of his life, he could never leave now.

Chapter Eight

Jennifer had read about Tom's exhibition in the paper, apparently it was a great success. She desperately wanted to see it, but she was anxious she might see Tom, and couldn't cope with that. The separation had been agony. She wanted, needed, to see him, but she loved him too much to hurt him any more by prolonging their relationship. 'This is mine to bear, not his,' she said to herself. He would recover – seeing her would only have put off the suffering. Writing to him everyday, brought some respite from her ache, but then she had destroyed the letters.

She thought of him continually. She had heard a song on the radio and the words played endlessly around and around in her head, *"For I know that love is more than just holding hands"*. Her fears seemed insignificant next to the pain of not being able to hold Tom and the ache of thinking he probably hated her. "This is so unfair", was her constant cry.

Twice she had started to drive up to where Tom lived once she got as far as the top of the hill above his house. She could see his house, but she drove her car over onto the grass verge and cried until there were no tears left, then she wearily turned her car around and went home. She glimpsed her red swollen face in the car mirror as she turned and wondered how she would explain it when she arrived home. When she did eventually make it home, it was nearly midnight. Her mother was quite frantic, clearly worried where she had been.

Jennifer walked straight past her and went to her room. She knew she was being unkind but she couldn't tell her mother what she had been doing, she would never understand, who would? She realised she was quite crazy, and that she was behaving atrociously to everyone, especially to her mother. She stayed in her room all the next day, her mother knocked on her door, but she said she couldn't talk; she was not feeling well and didn't want to see anyone. Her mother asked if she should call the doctor.

'No, just leave me alone, I don't want to see *anyone*.' Jennifer wondered how she was going to live with this pain; it hadn't eased in the slightest since she left Tom. 'How much longer.' She cried out.

Jennifer had held out as long as she was able, she was going to see his exhibition today. She would go to town after lunch and shop, at least that would be the excuse to her parents.

Jennifer was like a cat on a hot tin roof over lunch; her eyes hardly left the clock on the drawing room wall.

'What's troubling you, Jennifer, darling?' her mother asked, 'can't you tell me, talking may help, you seem very on edge, I only want to help, I won't be cross whatever it is, we have always been so close.'

'There's *nothing* wrong with me, I'm fine leave me alone; I'm not a child. Oh... I'm sorry Mummy, I know you are trying to be kind, it's merely that I don't want to miss the bus into town, that's all.'

'*The bus*! Take your car.'

'NO! Parking is a problem.' Jennifer didn't want to go in her car it was too noticeable. Tom might see her and she may not see him, no, it would be better on foot, wearing a headscarf and turning up her coat collar would give her some anonymity, blending into the crowd.

Eventually Jennifer was on the bus, and glad to be away from her mother's constant suffocating questions. The bus was full and she had to stand. She didn't mind because standing compelled her to focus on keeping her balance, rather than what was ahead this afternoon. She felt to be shaken and tossed in every direction as the bus manoeuvred its way through the busy Christmas traffic. It was a welcome distraction from the raging turmoil in her head. Her anxiety was destroying her ability to function.

Jennifer's immediate concern was that of accidentally bumping into Tom, and then what would she do. She couldn't even think about that. The sensible thing would have been to stay away from the exhibition, she knew that, but she had to see it. She was drawn like a moth to the flame; she would just have to pray that she didn't get burned.

Jennifer did what little shopping she had to do and then made her way to the gallery, deciding to hang around outside until closing time, and then sneak in to see Tom's work at the last minute, before they shut the doors. Perhaps that would bring him nearer; knowing what she saw was part of him. Sitting in a coffee bar across the road from the exhibition, she was able to view the entrance.

Suddenly he was there, on the other side of the road leaving the gallery, 'There's Tom he mustn't see me!' Her heart was pounding against her chest, she literally had to cling to the table to prevent her self running to him and leaping into his arms. She waited until he was out of sight, before she went across to the entrance; glancing at her watch, she saw there was still ten minutes before the official closing time. Only a couple of visitors were left in the gallery now.

Once inside Jennifer felt able to breathe again, sliding her headscarf off her head and loosening the collar of her coat, conscious that she was sweating.

At last able to view Tom's work, she gazed in wonder, quite overwhelmed. There was so much to look at. Her brain was desperately trying to absorb every scene and brush stroke in the short time there was left before closing.

She never imagined how dramatically different they would look exhibited and arranged professionally. When she had last seen any of his work it was in his garden stood against the hedge. These pictures were so beautiful – no – they were more than that, they were spiritual, they took one prisoner, capturing one's emotion. Yes, that was it; they captured emotions in a moment of time. They froze the moving image of eternity, and turned it into colours and form. The onlooker and the artist's heart were one.

She sat on a bench before her portrait, remembering vividly that afternoon when he started it, knowing then that she was in love and would never doubt it again. She knew at that instant, to stay was not possible and she had to leave him. No one else would see that torment in this face, but she could, and the tears began to spill from her eyes as she remembered.

She reached into her pocket for a handkerchief. Her whole body shook quietly as she tried to control herself. She couldn't help it; his work was breathtaking.

'That will always be my favourite, it will never be for sale.' She swung around at the sound, startled by the voice; it was Tom standing right behind her.

'TOM! I saw you go, I didn't mean this to happen. It's no good – I can't do this – I'm not strong enough,' and she bent forward her face in her hands. Tom walked around in front of her, crouched down, and took her in his arms.

'TOM, I'm sorry, please forgive me,' she said looking pleadingly into his eyes.

'Shush, you're in my arms that's all that matters to me, it has been living hell without you.'

'Tom, you don't understand, I'm... dying.'

'All that's past, we are together, that's everything.'

'No, no Tom, you don't understand, I didn't want to hurt you, but I'm too weak and selfish I can't keep this lie going, I'm dying and I have missed you so much.' He was holding her but his face was blank now.

'You're dying, what do you mean, I don't understand?'

'Tom, I have cancer, and perhaps at worst six months, at best eighteen. Anyway, we are talking about life that's measured out in months, not years, months, do you understand? I may be cured, but that is a long shot, that's all I can say, and to put that onto anyone is unfair.'

He held her by the shoulders at arms length and stared into her now swollen red eyes.

There were no words. He felt like a child, in a grown up world without any comprehension, but he wasn't a child this *was* a grown up world and nothing had prepared him for this, not in his wildest imagination had such a thought occurred to him.

He had never thought about her and her possible torment, he realised now, all his thoughts had been about himself and what he was suffering. He merely stared at this beautiful face; he was completely numb, all he could see was this innocence before him.

'That... it just, it just, can't be right, you must be mistaken.' She shook her head.

'I'm sorry Tom.' His expression was completely blank, she had longed for him to hold her, now she wanted to take this lost boy into *her* arms.

'I can't accept it, I can't.' He said and held her tightly.

'Everything all right Mr Jackson? It's just that I have to lock up,' said the caretaker coming reluctantly towards them, clearly he saw there was some problem.

'*What?* Oh, yes, yes, sorry Ray,' Tom said trying to deal with normality when there was none. He was in another world another time and dimension, he was quite unable to think. What on earth was he saying, nothing was "Alright", the plug had been pulled out, and his life was disappearing down the plughole.

Nothing had any solidity; it was all vapour evaporating before his eyes. "Lock up". What! What the bloody hell was he talking about, the place could fall down for all he cared. How could there be such disparity between feelings in such close physical proximity, didn't he know the world had ended where he was standing.

'Did you know you left your haversack in the office?'

'Err, yes, I came back for it, sorry, sorry about that, Ray.' Tom couldn't clear his head; his voice was in that other world, no longer under his control.

'You sure you're alright, Mr Jackson?'

'Yes, I'll collect my bag and go, thank you.' He got up and offered a hand to Jennifer; she grasped it and stood, clinging to him as they walked outside, it was dark now. He took her in his arms and kissed her.

'Here, fasten your collar, it's cold,' and he buttoned her coat and tenderly tied her scarf as if he was a loving father sending his child to school. He kissed her lightly once more on the lips.

'How are you travelling Jennifer? Oh, blast, I have still forgotten my haversack, just wait here a moment, I will dash back and pick it up, my wallet's in it. I'd forget my head if it wasn't screwed on. Don't you dare move from this spot.' Tom was only a moment, when he stepped out of the building once again, he saw Jennifer struggling with a young man who was clearly manhandling her, and trying to kiss her.

'Come on Jennifer, it's Christmas, you know you want to, we could go back to my flat.'

'Get off me, you're hurting me, leave me alone.' Tom set his haversack on the ground, ran down the few steps, took hold of the man by the shoulder and jerked him free of Jennifer, he stumbled back, only just managing to keep his balance.

'Who the hell are you?' The young man shouted at Tom. 'Come on then if you fancy your chances,' he barked, as he stepped forward swinging his fist at Tom, who instinctively ducked to one side and at the same time followed through with his own blow, striking him full force square in the face. There was a crunch of breaking bone.

The man fell to his knees, clasping his nose, blood pouring through his fingers.

'You madman, look what you have done to me, I'll have the law on you for this,' he screamed up at Tom.

'Don't be *pathetic*, Jeremy,' Jennifer said, with all the disdain she could manage. Tom took her arm, reached back up the steps to retrieve his haversack, and they walked off.

'*SLUT,*' he shouted after them. Tom was about to turn back, but Jennifer firmly tugged his arm.

'Ignore him Tom, he's not worth it.'

'What was all that about, do you know him?'

'Tom, can we forget about this? I don't want meeting you again to be spoiled by him.'

'As you wish, but he was lucky that I only hit him once, his sort make my blood boil. So how *did* you get here?

'I came on the bus, it's easier, no issues with the Christmas parking. That's not true, that wasn't the reason, I was nervous about coming in my car in case you saw it. You see I did try Tom. I didn't want to hurt you, I shouldn't have come at all.'

'Well you did. We'll go back to my room in Gosforth, we need to talk.'

'Tom, I am so sorry, I never meant to do this to you, it's unforgivable, it really is wicked.'

'Look, all I know is that I love you more than I imagined it possible to love another human being, and whatever life's got in store for me, I'm never letting go of you again. Do you hear me?' unexpectedly, he fiercely gripped her shoulders and shook her slightly. 'Every minute, from now on will be spent with you, that will be the whole of my life. Without you, there is nothing, I have been there and it was hell.'

Jennifer nodded; this is what she wanted too, just the two of them in *their* world, not like the other world, where time seemed infinite, the time in *their* world was finite.

Tom's digs were only a ten-minute bus ride away. They never spoke as the bus bumped and shook its way along the twists and turns of the city streets. She cuddled into him and he laid his cheek against her head.

'This is our stop, it's not far to walk.' He held her hand as she stepped from the bus, 'Careful.' Tom felt in his pocket for his keys, and they made their way across the road and up a scantily lit street to a dingy terrace house, sorely in need of painting. He put the key in the lock, opened the door, and showed Jennifer in. His landlady came out of her room immediately she heard their voices.

They started up the stairs, 'I don't allow female guests in men's rooms,' She shouted after him. Tom ignored her and they continued up to his room.

'Hoy, I'm talking to you.' Tom sighed wearily and turned back to her, managing, just, to contain his anger. Awe flipping heck, he thought, I don't need this stupid woman's self-righteousness at this moment, especially when she isn't married to the bloke she lives with.

'Right now, I'm going to my room, but it will be free as soon as I can pack my case, so sort out my bill,' Tom said angrily, then he gently moved Jennifer on up the stairs. 'Sorry about this Jennifer, but I won't be heartbroken to be out of this place, I can tell you. This is awful, dragging you all over town, but there is a pub just down the road I'll get a room there.'

'Tom, I'm sorry, I'm only trouble for you, that will cost you even more money, I'll just go...' He stifled her words pressing his lips to hers, and then stood back.

'No you won't, don't ever say those words again. I have sold most of my pictures in the exhibition, and you would not believe how much I have made, so I was leaving here whether-or-not.' Tom packed while Jennifer sat at the table, it was a dump, she had never been in a place like it, and it was filthy, worse than Tom's house where they had met. They came downstairs and the landlady was there with his bill, which she thrust indignantly at him.

'You'll have te pay till the end of the week.'

He looked at the total written at the bottom, 'Phew, are you sure it's not until the end of the year.'

'Good digs are expensive in the "Toon".'

'By the look of these prices, I imagine they are, not that I have experienced any.'

'Cheeky blighter.' Ahhh what the heck, he thought, what does money matter, she can have the lot, for all I care at this minute. He took out his wallet and paid her.

'Good riddance,' was her parting shot. He was at a loss to know how he restrained himself from knocking her block off; Jennifer sensed his pause and tugged him forward. With his haversack over his shoulder, his case in one hand and Jennifer in the other, they made their way down to the "Red Lion". It was just starting to rain; they walked in to be welcomed by a blazing fire.

'Have you any rooms for my wife and I?'

'Whey-aye, how lang for like?'

'Oh, err, one week,' he said, looking at Jennifer, she shrugged her shoulders.

'Diven't a nah ye from somewhere? A 'ave a good memory for faces like, wait a minute... ye're that famous artist bloke, 'ave seen int' gazette, hang on now... Jacksun, whey-aye that's it Jacksun.' Tom was quite distracted for a moment.

'I don't know about famous, but my name is Jackson.'

'Hoy Lilly, we've got that famous artist Mr Jacksun and his lass tee stay, you knaa, we've been tee his exhibition, by heck, there was a couple of muckle big pictures there, come and say hello.' His wife popped her head around the corner and smiled at them.

'Pleased tee meet you I'm sure, I'm Missus Liddell.' Tom and Jennifer were compelled to shake hands.

'Whey, I recognise yor lass tee. Whey-man, it was yor picture on the waal, wasn't it?' The landlord said and Jennifer smiled in acknowledgement.

'You're very kind, but could we see the room, my wife is a little tired.'

'Whey-aye, you can ha the best room in the hoose, here let me teck ya case for ya, bonny lad, haway follow me.' The landlord took them upstairs to the room and it was indeed a very pleasant room, right next door to the bathroom.

'You diven't soond like a local, ye soond a bit posh like, where ar' ye from?'

'Actually, I'm a Newcastle lad born and bred.' Please, please stop talking, the room is perfect, now leave us, Tom silently pleaded, I'm going mad.

'Well ah nivvor. Just call oot if ye needs oot. Breakfast's from siven till nine, and ye get some sleep hinny, ye looks worn oot.'

'Thank you very much,' Tom said, virtually pushing the man out of the room, desperately trying to bring closure to the benign chatter.

'What a flipping nightmare, I thought he was never going to go. Sorry about that Jen.'

'It's perfectly alright Tom, the man was only trying to be kind.'

'Here let me take your coat.' Jennifer removed her coat and passed it to him, 'I'll hang them over this chair they are damp. Now tell me all, you have no idea how much I have longed to hear your voice.'

'Tom, I'm sorry for hurting you,' she lowered her eyes and spoke softly, 'believe me it tore my heart in two. I wanted to spare you; I was trying to be unselfish, I needed you, more than you can imagine.' She paused, unable to continue. Tom took hold of her hands, but said nothing, giving her time to say all she wanted or needed to say. 'Now all that we have been through is undone, suffering for nothing, time squandered. I hate and despise myself for saying this, after I have struggled and tormented myself, resolved not to, Tom... I love you. How many times I wanted to say that to you. That day when you left me on the beach, I was trying to be so strong. All that time *wasted* and we have so little to waste.'

He leant forward taking her in his arms and shook his head slightly, in understanding at their shared regret. Without letting go of her, he slipped off his shoes. Still holding her hand, he sat down on the edge of the bed, and tugged her towards him. Jennifer looked at him for a moment, and then sat down beside him.

'I didn't realise; I thought I had found what a life needs to make it complete, only to lose it. The completeness you brought was torn away. Some people never find what we have. Oh they long for it, perhaps dream of it, but there is a heavy price to be paid, and I am frightened that I might not be up to it.' Jennifer kissed him tenderly and they lay down. He could see her looking at his forehead; she ran her finger lightly over the scars.

'Whatever have you done to cause these awful scars?'

'Oh, I fell, nothing really.'

'They are dreadful, you will be marked for life.'

'Jen, if you only knew the truth of those words.'

She rested her lips against his ear; they were warm and sensual. 'Make love to me Tom...' She whispered and pressed into him, as if trying to merge their two beings into one spiritual mass and so give them greater strength to face what must be faced. He felt the warmth of her body, her urgency, she gasped, his hand brushed against her breast as his fingers fumbled with the buttons of her blouse. She responded eagerly, frantically undoing his shirt. Her breathing was jagged. He could feel the swell of her breasts against his chest. She lifted her body to enable him to remove her blouse and to release her bra, and the zip of her skirt – he gradually stilled and lay back drawing her nakedness to his chest.

'What is it? She panicked, 'Tom, have I done something wrong?'

'No – no, nothing like that, I want you – I need you, but this is madness.' Her eyes were filled with hurt and rejection, she tried to pull away, but he held her tightly. 'Jen – I want you – more than life, there is nothing but you, no heaven or earth no beginning or end, only you, don't ever doubt that. These are not merely a lover's silken words, that fall from the lips of desire and disappear in the morning light. These words come from a heart, which puts you first, before my needs. The truth is Jen, I can't be any different, it's just the way I feel about you. I can't explain it, I don't understand it, it is all new to me. I feel powerless, this feeling controls me, if you are cut, I will bleed I am convinced of that.'

'You think that I don't understand? Believe me I do. I'm sure people will mock us for talking like this, but all that means is they have never really loved.'

'Jen, my whole life has been about me, Tom the special one, now it's about you and this would be foolish. Think for a moment, what if you got pregnant...?' She relaxed into his arms now and cried afresh at the cruelty. She wanted his baby, that's what love was, but she might be dead before any baby could be given life. She wanted to be a mother, her body trembled, she wanted to be Tom's wife she wanted, she wanted. Her crying was inconsolable now. Tom held her. What a diabolical mess, this is not fair, not fair at all, he thought as he shook his head repeatedly in disbelief.

Gradually Jennifer's sobbing stilled and they lay still, merely holding each other. When she had calmed, Tom eased his arm free, kissed her, and slid his legs over the edge of the bed. He leant forward resting his forearms on his knees and hung his head in despair, staring mindlessly at the floor.

Jennifer clung to his waist, he turned to her and gently touched her face, 'I'm sorry Jen.'

'What for Tom?' she whispered.

'For making your life more complicated.'

'No! Are you saying you want to go? Tom, please?' Her voice trembled.

'Jen, you can put that thought out of your mind, that will never be the case. It's not about me, it's about you; you are my life. As I have just said, I have never had to think of anyone else before, I was the golden boy, and everyone ran after me. I killed my mother; slaving all hours for me, she was so proud, you wouldn't believe it. I'm a selfish git, Jen, but knowing you has touched something inside me, and now... I'm not important at all. I will give up everything, I pray, if there is a God, that He puts your suffering onto me and I will take it gladly and be thankful.'

'I don't know this man you talk of Tom. The man I know is filled with love, his eyes speak only of kindness and selflessness, and I love him.' She slid her legs over the edge of the bed and sat next to him resting her head on his shoulder, he put his arm around her and drew her to him.

'Remember the swallows we watched? We'll be like them, we'll swoop and soar, this is our season, whatever the time of year it is, we will be here until autumn. I'm sure they never think about tomorrow, each new day is a joy filled with wonder. We are all going to die sometime, you and I will live a long and full life in the time we have. We must live every second, only we can do that, no one else can do it for us. This applies to everyone not just us, but they don't know it, we are the lucky ones.' He turned to face her and she pressed her lips to his...

His lips move lightly, caressing her cheek and her eyelids; then he cupped her face in his hands and stared into her eyes, after a moment he said, 'Do you know, Jen, swallows pair for life?'

'Do they?'

'Yes.'

They lay back on the bed and she snuggled once again into his chest. Jennifer lay for some minutes in silence, sensing that Tom was struggling to say something.

'Jen... may I ask about your illness, this one time, then we will move on?'

Jennifer closed her eyes and was quiet. He felt her press closer to him, eventually in a soft voice she said, 'It's what they call, a lymphoma. I first noticed a lump on my neck,' she touched her neck where the lump had been. 'It's not a single disease, but rather a group of several closely related cancers, apparently. It's in stage two now, that's when the cancer is found in two or more places in my chest. There are five or six stages, it's not something they can operate on and remove, it's in me, all rather grim. That's about all I know, apart from... let's not go there, it all sounds pants to me. I don't really understand it very well; I listen but can't seem to take it in. Once the big "C" is mentioned, one's brain seems to close down.'

'Yes... I imagine it does,' was all he said, no questions. Jennifer felt a tear run from his face onto her cheek, she held her lip between her teeth to stifle any reaction. The tear traced its way down the side of her nose and dripped off her chin. It seemed poignant to her that she was able to be physically part of that tear. They were still undressed and the touch of his skin against hers brought an intimacy she found immensely comforting.

She had not felt so at peace, since she last saw Tom. This was right she knew it was, and she kissed his chest.

'Will you marry me Jen?' She was shaken, she hadn't expected this, but she managed not to show her surprise by any startled movement. In fact, in the space before she answered, she realised that it was the most natural thing in the world to ask.

'Yes, I will, but Tom, you don't have to do that, it's too much to ask of you.'

'There will never be anyone else, only you, that's forever. I meant it when I said I will be with you every minute, nothing will separate us.'

'If I am going to stay with you, I must ring my father and mother; they will worry if I don't go home tonight. I'll have to make some excuse. Daddy would have wanted a big wedding. I'm an only one, such a wedding won't be possible because of time limitations, he will be disappointed.'

'What are they like?'

'Who, mummy, and daddy?'

'Yes, your mum and dad, will we get on?'

'It's not going to be easy. Daddy's a successful executive and his world spins how he wants it to, this has been difficult for him. He actually... owns the paper I work for.'

'Difficult for him, I imagine it was. Finding out your child is seriously ill must be the worst news a parent can get.'

'Let's not think on that this evening. Can we go for a walk Tom? And I'll cover up this skinny excuse for a body.' She made to move, but he tightened his grip.

'I want you to know, Jen, no trite words; *I* think you are beautiful. It might be that love sandpapers over faults, who knows, I hope so. When you have as many faults as me, you need as much help as you can get.'

Jen laughed, 'They say love is blind, where are my spectacles?'

'I've hidden them,' Tom said and kissed her again. 'Come on; let's go for that walk, while I'm still ahead. I have some shopping to do. Tonight you will be my wife and tomorrow I'll look into getting a marriage licence, we'll find the nearest Registrar's Office and you will be "Missus" *Jacksun.*' They both laughed.

'Do you know Tom how wonderful that makes me feel. I was as miserable as sin when I left the house this morning, now I am happy, happy. Come on let's get ready and go.'

It was true, Tom thought as they dressed, even though on the face of it, life was pretty grim; he knew exactly how Jennifer felt. This was better than being apart and they would make the most of this time together. He supposed that the torment of the last weeks was part of the happiness now. As they walked, they actually laughed stopping every few yards to hug and kiss, yes, they would live each moment to the full, he could die tomorrow that's the reality of life. They strolled into the town centre. The Christmas lights were up, and they were not the only ones laughing, there was a general air of excitement. Christmas was just around the corner.

'We have a hurdle to cross and we may as well get it over quickly,' Jennifer pointed out.

'Oh heck, what's that?'

'I'm still thinking about mummy and daddy.'

'I suppose that will have to be faced.'

'I can put them off for a while, but sooner or later, they are going to want to know what's going on, and, I will want them at my wedding, I simply don't know what's best. Tom, I want my father to give me away, it might only be at the registrar office but I want a proper wedding.'

'Whatever you want I'm fine with, there's no problem there.'

'I'm afraid there is,' Tom stopped walking and turned to her, wondering what she was going to "Hit him with", 'Like you Tom I want to spend every moment together, every second is precious, and they are going to struggle with that.'

'Ah, mmm, I see what you mean, I won't compromise on that, I will be with you every moment. I suppose you live with them, I mean you don't have a flat or anything?'

'No.'

'This is "Pants", as you put it.'

'I will have to take you to meet them and tell them we are to be married.'

'Oh flip, wow, I rather imagined that it was just you and me; I didn't take all this onboard, stupid or what. I didn't even think of my lot, to be fair it's all been a bit instant, that's the sixties for you, the world of instant is here.'

'Mother and Father are a touch more old fashioned I'm afraid, the sixties love and peace, with its liberal dashing of free sex, has not arrived at Manor Park.'

'Where?'

'Manor Park, that's where Mother and Father live.'

'And the shocks keep coming. I came from Waterloo Terrace, no manor and you stayed clear of the park for fear of weirdos,' he laughed, 'I don't know what I'm laughing at, it must be nerves.'

'You are funny Tom; it's just the name of a house. Tom, it's good to be with you again, and hear your laughter,' and she reached up and kissed his cheek.

Chapter Nine

Tom purchased what was needed; fortunately, Boots the chemists was still open, making the most of the Christmas trade. They wandered along Northumberland Street looking in the shop windows, a man was selling hot pies, and Tom bought two. They continued walking as the ate. It was cold, their breath condensed on the frosty air. He affectionately wiped the gravy from Jennifer's chin; her pie had all but exploded when she bit into it. Who cared, they laughed as they walked.

'Come on, we better be getting back, or we'll miss the evening meal.' They didn't have long to wait the buses seemed reasonably regular. Soon they were on the bus and bumping along merrily to the stop near the Red Lion. People were already eating, so they went straight into the restaurant area.

A very formal waitress in black with a pristine starched white apron, asked what room they were in, and ushered them to their table, in a corner, it felt quite intimate, there were only ten tables, and three were vacant. The landlord came to them with a wine menu.

'Shall we have Mateus Rose, not because it's special, simply it's the only one I know. Sorry, not much of a wine buff.'

'You told me that when we had our first meal together, remember?'

'So I did.'

'Do you know, I was famished that night, Tom, you seem to make me hungry, it's ages since I really felt like eating.'

'Me too, I have worked off that pie we had in "The Toon".'

'Yes, I noticed that you had lost the puppy fat you were carrying when we first met.'

'I'll have you know, this is finely toned muscle.'

'Of course, it is,' she laughed. 'Remember there are no secrets now, I have seen your naked body, how risqué it seems, to be able to say that.'

'Ah, that's the end of my sex life, it's enough to put anyone off.'

'Perhaps I could give you a second chance,' they both laughed, and he squeezed her hand.

Tom ordered steak and Jennifer ordered spaghetti bolognese. Jennifer wanted to pay, 'Jen I told you I had made a ridiculous amount from my paintings, I kid you not, I made eight thousand pounds, give or take, that's nearly three times what I made in a year teaching, for a load of old tat.'

'Tom, don't forget I have seen your work, and it is outstanding, you are going to be a very famous artist, that is for sure.'

'Ah, you're just biased, but whatever, I'm not complaining.'

The meal duly came, a large steak with potatoes and a selection of vegetables, they both looked startled at the size of their plates simultaneously saying, 'Wow.'

'I can't say I'm over keen on Italian food, too much tomato for me, meat and two veg' man, that's me.'

'I like to try different things, but I'm not much of a cook, I'm afraid.'

'So your poor mum does the donkey work in your house, oh I forgot, you spend most of your time at the chippy?'

'Ha, not quite.'

Their chatter continued, and Tom asked about her mother and father, 'Sooooo, what about your ma and pa, how are we going to play that?'

'You'll *have* to meet them.'

'I guess so, but when?' Tom said nervously.

'I would like to get it over with as soon as possible, so we can move on. I could ring Father, as I said earlier, but really, that would be the coward's way out. Tom... could we go tonight, would you mind terribly?'

'Oh heck Jen, that's my appetite gone.' she laughed.

'Mummy may reluctantly understand, but it will be a problem for Daddy, he likes to be in

81

control of anything to do with him. He won't be happy when I introduce you. I told them I was going shopping this morning, which was partly the truth. He will assume I had arranged to see you and deceived him, *and* then tell him we are getting married. He is not going to take it well. Really, the air needs to be cleared as soon as possible.'

'To be fair to him, if my daughter went shopping and came back married, it might cause me some consternation too. Why is everything so convoluted?'

'Yes, I suppose so, listen, Tom, what do you say, could we go there tonight and get it over with?'

'Then what?'

'We will just have to play it by ear, Tom.'

'We will save money on the dessert, 'cause I have definitely lost my appetite now, come on let's just finish off and face the music. I had better change first and put a clean shirt on at least, it will have to be these jeans, I'm afraid, and I feel such a scruff. You manage to look classy, even in your tat, how do you do it?'

'Come on, what you are wearing is the least of our problems. I can pick up my car when we are there and leave it in the car park here.'

Once again, they were on the bus, Tom could not believe how nervous he was when he woke this morning, he hadn't imagined in his wildest dreams what the day would hold.

If he had not forgotten his haversack, his life would have been entirely different. It struck him how delicately balanced life was, he squeezed Jennifer's hand, and she smiled at him. It wasn't that far to Jennifer's home, on the outskirts of Gosforth, off the A1 northbound.

When Jennifer's home came into view, Tom moaned, 'Oh flipping heck, tell me this is not your house, and actually this is where the Duke of Northumberland lives, it's blinking enormous, "Oh! You are so funny Tom, it's just the name of a house",' Tom said, imitating Jennifer's accent as he repeated her earlier announcement. 'Jen, why didn't you warn me?'

Tom was facing a Victorian mansion with big wrought iron gates and along gravelled drive, bordered by rhododendrons, which was lit by converted gas lamps. 'There's enough stone in the outbuildings to build our whole street.'

'Sorry Tom, I never thought to mention it. My great-grandfather built it. He was involved in coal mining.'

'Oh a pitman, was he?'

'Err, not quite,' she smiled.

'Be sure to tell your dad I'm a rich, famous artist, lay it on thick, don't mention I'm a bum. Tell him I'm avant-garde if he looks at my clothes.' Jennifer laughed again.

'Tom you are stellar,' she said. They walked in; she felt to be dragging him. 'Faint heart and all that jazz.'

'Ah, Miss Jennifer.'

'Hello, Mr Warwick.'

'His Lordship and her Ladyship are in the drawing room.'

'This is Mr Jackson, Mr Warwick.'

'Pleased to meet you Sir, Lady Jenifer,' he said bowing his head.

'*"L-a-d-y Jennifer!"* Ohhh, Jen, you are kidding me. You have landed me right in it.' I'm not "Sir" anything I'm Tom Jackson, just plain Tom from Waterloo Terrace. Who was that person? – No, please no, not the butler. I am way out of my depth here. Even the traumatic seizure I'm now experiencing has not been able to prevent my brain firing into to panic mode, and unleashing all the fear my psychic has stored up for just such an occasion. what's all this Ladyship business about?'

'Oh don't fuss, Tom.'

'Oh don't fuss, Tom, Ha. have you ever thought of taking up counselling? With your calming approach, should be a natural,''

'Come on it's along here.' Jennifer led the way along the corridor to the drawing room. She put her head around the door; her mother and father were watching the television.

Her mother looked up, 'Ah, Jennifer it's you, we were beginning to wonder where you were, you might have rung, darling, it's ten o'clock now. I have been worried, you usually call us if you are going to be late.'

Tom looked around; he couldn't have been more at a loss if he had walked into Buckingham Palace. He was unable to assimilate all the pictures and bits of objet d'art. His front room at Waterloo Terrace would have fitted into the fireplace.

To perfect moment suave, sophisticated entrance; Tom stumbled over a curled up edge of the carpet, making him feel more like a circus clown than the suitor for a peer of the realm's daughter. I will kill you when I get you out of here, Jen. Which is supposing I can ever find my way out, he thought, this place is a maze.

'Sorry Mummy – I have brought someone with me, this is Tom.' They both looked now. Jennifer's father stood, Tom couldn't read his expression at all, I wouldn't want to play poker against this guy, he thought. The fellow was not at ease though; Tom noticed that he was nervously twisting a signet ring around and around his little finger. He was wearing a shabby wool jumper; the sort that toffs wear, which has been handed down through the generations since William the Conqueror was a boy.

Tom was sure if he'd worn such a thing, his mother would have died of shame, highlighting their financial state, a declaration to all the neighbours that she couldn't afford to buy her kids decent clothes. However, for the "Nobs", it was almost a badge of right; to emphasise they had been around for years. Jennifer's mother wore blue slacks, and a matching cardigan with a white blouse, and the obligatory set of pearls. It was the same casual way that Jennifer dressed, understated, but classy, which seemed effortless, as if it was all part of the upper-crust's "DNA", and he had never twigged it.

He had never given Jennifer's background a thought. Her accent alone should have rung warning bells. I should have realised that she didn't come from anywhere near *Waterloo Terrace*, what a "Numpty", Tom thought, shaking his head at his utter stupidity. He had never considered beyond what they were doing at any given moment. The time spent together had consumed his thinking. Little did he imagine on those sunny days laughing playing by the sea, that such a myopic view of life would have to be the model for the rest of their lives together.

'This is Tom; I'm sure you will have read about him in the papers. He has had a very successful exhibition in the town. He's an artist; we have known each other for some time.'

'Can't say I have,' said her father, dismissively.

Brill', great start, he loves me, flashed across Tom's mind.

'Pleased to meet you, nice house you have here.' Awe flipping heck, that was so

Waterloo Terrace, Tom *cringed* as the words left his lips.

'Hmm, take a seat, I'm not terribly interested in art, apart from an investment, how much do yours go for?'

'Err, around the thousand pound mark.' Tom allowed himself a slight exaggeration, her father didn't seem impressed, 'For a small picture,' he added quickly.

'Hmm.'

'Daddy, Mummy, we have come to tell you that Tom and I are getting married.' The announcement was received with a silence, which could have been cut with a knife. Jennifer's father eventually broke the silence.

'Oh you are, are you?' His words sounded to Tom like a challenge and Tom's hackles were instantly raised. If he wants a fight, I'm up for it. I'm not into bowing and scraping, Lord or not, makes no difference. This is none negotiable.

'Yes, that's right and very soon.' That didn't go well, her father stood up and so did Tom.

'You're not *pregnant*! This is *your* fault,' he turned to Jennifer's mother.

'I beg your pardon, Father! Thank you for the high regard in which you clearly hold me. I am not pregnant.'

'Now, now, Peter, let us hear what Jennifer and Tom have to say.' They sat down again.

'Have you had anything to eat, can I ask Warwick to bring you something?' Jennifer's mother said, in an attempt to lighten the mood.

'Thank you, Lady...'

'Call me Carolyn, in fact, most people call me Bunny, a throwback to school days.' Clearly, she was nervous too.

'Thank you Lady Carolyn, we have already eaten.' Tom thought he would have to grow into Bunny, the only bunnies he knew, hung in the butcher's window.

'Perhaps some tea?' Jennifer's father looked on in disdain.

'Yes, that would be kind Mummy,' Jennifer jumped in. 'Look, Daddy it's no good us beating about the bush, we all know what's ahead of us. Tom and I are in love, and want to spend what time we have together, surely you can understand that Daddy.'

'Have you been to university?' Her dad asked, out-of-the-blue.

'Yes, what has that to do with anything.' Tom asked, struggling to control his temper.

'Which one?'

'Daddy, unlike you, he didn't go to Oxford, he went to Newcastle, he's a rabid socialist and has posters of Harold Wilson all over his walls.'

'I have! You know more than I do,' Tom said, momentarily distracted by Jennifer's quick wit.

'Don't be facetious girl. Hoping to get your hands on some money are you?'

'Right! I don't have to take this, come on Jen,' Tom stood, he was furious.

'DADDY! That is absolutely outrageous, Tom didn't know I had any money, and if he had, I know that it would not have made the slightest difference. You either apologise, or I leave with Tom now, and that will hurt me very much because I won't be back.' Jennifer's support calmed Tom slightly and took the heat out of the situation. 'I'm waiting for you Father.' Jennifer stood ridged arms folded, tapping her foot. It was a wonder his face didn't freeze over by the iced stare she was giving him

'Look, Jennifer, this has been a horrendous time for me.'

'I don't believe this, what about your daughter, how do you think she has been feeling?'

'I meant – it has been a difficult time for us all.'

'Sure you did – come on Jen this is hopeless.'

'Father, I'm still waiting.'

'I apologise, but you must understand...'

'Oh, I understand all right.'

'TOM! Will you both sit down?' They all sat down again. 'This is difficult for us all. I love Tom.'

'Now then Mr Jackson, I wonder if you are the cause of my, normally affectionate daughter's withdrawal over the past weeks?' Asked Jennifer's mother as she narrowed her eyes, and smiled kindly at him.

'Tom was wholly innocent Mother; I knew I loved him and that he loved me, but I didn't want to cause him any more hurt. We met when I went to recuperate by the sea. I hoped and prayed that it was just a holiday romance and we would get over it, but I can't. I have tried but I can't. Every moment without Tom has made me feel worse than I already did. We met serendipitously today, neither of us knew it was going to happen, and neither of us has had a change of heart, in the time we have been separated. Tom is everything to me, in one day, he has transformed my pain into joy, and I need him, as much as the air I breathe.'

'Sentimental nonsense,' her father scoffed.

'Is that how you feel about Mummy?'

'Don't be impertinent.'

'Jen, this is hopeless,' Tom said, flicking his hand in disgust.

'I *will* have my say, Tom. We... I know this will be hard for you, both and I'm truly sorry. Tom and I wish it could have been different. We all know what cards we've been dealt, and we intend to make to most of it. We are going to get married as soon as we can, and... until then... we will live together.'

'WHAT!'

'Sorry Daddy, I am twenty-two, it's not what I would have wanted as I have just said, but this is going to happen. Try – to see it from our point of view. Daddy, I want a wedding, and I want you to give me away.'

'Peter, if they are to be married anyway. I don't want to be separated from Jennifer; I need to see her. Could they not live at the Lodge, for the time being, *please* Peter?'

'I am not happy about this Jennifer, not at all; this is very selfish of you. Whatever will our friends think.' Jennifer laid her hand on Tom's leg, hopefully, to deflect any reaction.

'So – can they stay at the Lodge, Peter?' Jennifer's mother pleaded; there was a hiatus in the swirling tension. Jennifer held Tom's arm, she was genuinely frightened that Tom would hit her father. Her father seemed oblivious to the hurtful, selfishness of his general attitude.

'If they must, but I am heartbroken about this; indeed, I never thought a daughter of mine would be so disrespectful.'

Ah, here comes the tea,' Lady Carolyn said before Tom could explode. 'Set it down there, Warwick, I will see to it.' The butler set the tray down on the coffee table and left. 'Milk and sugar, Tom.'

'Yes, just as it comes, thank you.' There was a moment of calm, while the formality of serving the tea was undertaken.'

'Are we to be told of your arrangements for tonight?' Jennifer's father asked in a sarcastic tone.

Tom was proving as much of a challenge as her father, she thought. She placed her foot on his before he reacted and said, 'Tom and I will be staying at the Red Lion in Gosforth.'

'So Lady Jennifer Dunwoody will be spending the night in a pub, how absolutely perfect, what more could a father want.'

Tom's eyes *and* cheeks bulged as he tried to prevent himself spraying his mouthful of tea over everyone; he turned towards Jennifer at this latest revelation that the girl he was going to marry, was not just plain Jen, the Beachcomber, but Lady Jennifer. She determined not to look at him. At least this new shock to his system had put him at a loss for words, which was helpful. Jennifer was almost compelled to smile at the expression on Tom's face, but this was not the moment for laughter.

'Daddy, I think if we work together, without aggression *or* sarcasm,' she glared at her father, 'we will all benefit. Nothing is "Normal", who knows how long I will have. What time there is, will be for Tom and I and I want us *all* to do more than make the best of it. I really think it can be better than that, but we will not if we continue to snipe at each other. I want to consider you both, and I would like you to consider both of us too, please.'

'Jennifer's right Peter, we must all work with each other, I am sure we would all wish things were different. So you are staying with Tom tonight, would you like to come and have dinner with us tomorrow night, Tom, say seven?'

'It's – up to you Jennifer, my exhibition finishes tomorrow, but I won't have to pack up until Monday.'

'We would love you to come too, Mummy, is that all right with you, Daddy?'

'Hmm.'

'So that's a yes then,' Jennifer said, staring at her father.

'Perhaps Tom, we could go to your exhibition together tomorrow, would you mind?' asked her mother. Tom adjusted his seating position, suddenly he was on the back-foot.'

'Err – certainly.'

'Thank you Mother, that is kind, I will pick you up. Will you come too, Daddy?'

'I will take your mother, then you will not be tied.' There was a moment of silence while the other three players tried to assimilate this offer.

Then Tom spoke, 'Thank you, Sir, that would probably be best. Do you know where it is?'

'I may have glimpsed something about it in the paper.'

'Just in case, it's at the Collinson Gallery, off the Haymarket,' Jennifer said.

'I think we should be going Jennifer it is nearly eleven thirty.' They stood up, and Jennifer hugged her mother, the moment was awkward with her father, in the end, Jennifer simply looked at him and gave a slight nod. Tom nodded to them both and thanked Jennifer's mother for asking him to dinner.

'I will have to get some things from my room first, do you mind if I show Tom my room, Mummy?'

'No, by all means, darling.'

'Huh,' her father grunted and went to his cigarette box. Tom was doing his best to ignore any provocation, but he was struggling. Thank goodness, Jen was not leaving him alone with them, though in truth, her mother seemed very lovely, he thought.

'This is very small,' Tom said when Jennifer showed him into her room.'

'Do you think so? I know there are bigger rooms than mine, but I liked this one.'

'Jen, you are ace; I was joking, our house wasn't this big.'

'Oh, I see, forgive me I'm a bit slow on the uptake.'

'Come here you nutcase and give me a hug. Thanks for keeping tight hold of my reins, I could have made a complete fool of myself down there, boy did it come close.'

'I never noticed.'

'Liar.' They both laughed. Jen packed a bright red suitcase, saying this would do, for now, there was no point in taking too many cases until where they were going to live was more solidity.

Chapter Ten

Tom closed the front door of Manor Park behind him and breathed a sigh of relief as they walked down the front steps. He was sure that this was what it would feel like to be stepping out of Durham jail, into the fresh air, having escaped the death sentence. He asked Jennifer where her car was, taking his hand, she led him around to what looked as if it had once been the stable block, to a pair of heavy looking large blue doors, and proceeded to tug at one of them.

'Here let me,' Tom said, Jennifer was clearly struggling to open it.

'Thanks Tom, I forgot you are an expert with doors that stick.' They both smiled.

Once he'd opened it, he asked, 'Are there any lights in here?' Tom felt along the wall, 'okay, I have it, that's better,' and the space was immediately illuminated by bright fluorescent lights. Jennifer unlocked the boot of her car and Tom pushed her suitcase in.

'I'll close up once you're out, you stay in the car Jen, there are some flurries of snow in the air. It might be a good idea to put the roof up.'

'Yes, I think open top motoring may not be the best form of travel tonight. If you can just give me a little help with the roof, thanks, it's fairly easy, can you get that side?' Tom helped her tug the folding roof into place. It fastened at the front head rail with two toggles, which he clipped into place.

Whilst they were securing the roof, Jennifer unsettled Tom, 'You seem a natural with cars, Tom.'

'Oh, that seemed pretty straightforward, perhaps I am.'

'Glad to hear it, because the first thing you are going to do is learn to drive.'

'*What!* You are joking.'

'No, I am not, I will teach you.'

'Are you mad, you might get killed, are you qualified?'

'All you need is a provisional licence and I will teach you the rest. There is a Second World War aerodrome not far from your house, where people go to practice, lots of room until you get the hang of it.'

'But Jen.'

'But me no buts, that's what is going to happen.' With that Jennifer climbed into the Vitesse; Tom simply stood with a blank expression scratching his head. She had to turn the engine over a couple of times before it started, clearly the engine was cold, it fired up, roared, and she drove out in a cloud of exhaust fumes. Tom closed the heavy double doors behind her and jumped into the passenger seat, 'Burrr, it's freezing,' he said rubbing his hands together. I will have to treat myself to some gloves, driving gloves by the sound of it.'

Jennifer reached over and kissed him, 'Have you any idea how happy I am Mr Jackson?'

'To be with a handsome rugged dish like me, of course you're happy.'

Jen laughed, 'Do you know what, that's just what you are to me.'

'Oh heck, that backfired, but you're seeing me at my best, in the dark, I better marry you quick before daylight.' She laughed again.

The traffic was quite light now; it was almost midnight, as they neared the Red Lion.

'So,' said Tom, 'I am to marry a Lady, you kept that very quiet, a wealthy Lady at that. That puts a whole different complexion on things.'

'What! What do you mean?'

'Clearly there is the matter of a dowry.'

'You frightened me there, don't do that.'

'You, frightened, you should have been in my pants in the last couple of hours or so.'

'Ha, now there's a thought to send a shiver down a young girl's spine, that will be the start of the dowry.'

He laughed, 'Don't spare the horses.' The Red Lion was in darkness when they arrived, apart from a light in the entrance. As they walked across the car park, Tom said, 'I hope we are not locked out, and have to return to your castle and throw ourselves on the mercy of your father. No, we are in luck, the door's not locked.'

'Tom, I *don't* live in a castle.'

'Give over, I have seen smaller castles, than your house.' Jennifer laughed and leant into his arm.

They quickly went up to their room. Tom helped Jennifer off with her coat kissing her neck, she gasped and turned to face him, taking his cold face in her hands and touching her nose to his, 'Love you, Mr J,' she said. 'Tom, I'm actually very nervous.'

'Nervous – what about?'

'Well... you know.'

'Ah.'

'I know you will think this, a bit pathetic, but I have never done this before, it was different this afternoon, it all just happened no planning, short of thinking time. Glad you had your brain in gear, actually....' she paused, 'when I had my treatment, they mentioned something about it affecting my fertility. I didn't pay any attention because that wasn't an issue.'

'Ah, I see,' and he held her. Then he lightened the moment, holding her at arm's length and smiling, 'Naturally you realise that

I am an accomplished lothario, you have met my last conquest – Dolly – the dog, remember the wet kisser?'

'Oh.'

'The fact is, the right girl simply didn't come along, the swinging sixties never seem to be happening where I was. *Not*, that is, until I was sitting on a seat in the sun, minding my own business one summer evening – and was seduced by a bikini clad wanton wench, who assaulted me in a pub,' she smiled. 'My trouble is, Jen, I'm a romantic, remember, you told me that day at Bamburgh when we watched the cricket. Come to think of it, you attacked me that day too.'

'You liar Tom Jackson, it was you who kissed me, *that day,*' and she pushed him back onto the bed and fell on top of him.'

'Was, it? Well I never,' and he kissed her again and tumbled her off him, holding her by her wrists, pinioning her arms above her head. 'Now I have you trapped, ma beauty. Ha, ha, and subject to ma wicked ways, ha, ha, shipmate,' he said with his inimitable version of a Long John Silver accent. Jennifer squirmed and laughed as he tickled her.

'I submit, I submit, you weigh a ton.' Tom kissed her again and ran his lips lightly up her neck to her ear.

'Ahhhh, now you have sapped all my strength,' Jennifer gasped. 'I will have to scream for help from our friendly landlord.'

'No! Not that, anything but that, a slow death by endless chatter,' and he released her, she was still laughing, when someone knocked on the wall.

'Oh heck!' Tom put his finger across his lip, 'shush you'll get us evicted.'

'What a pair we are,' she whispered, trying to control her hysterics, 'if Mother and Father only knew,' she laughed, 'they probably wouldn't believe that we hadn't spent that whole holiday in bed.'

'Come here woman, did I tell you I love you?

'Do you know Tom I feel as if I have always known you. It's odd, as if I am living something that has already been played out. It's the most frightfully bizarre feeling.'

'It's blinking playing out quickly, it's one o'clock now. Are you going to the bathroom first?'

'Just as you like, Tom, sorry, I haven't got anything wildly exciting to wear, I usually wear pyjamas.'

'What! No slinky black number?'

'Afraid not, sorry. What if we go for a more *basic* sleeping attire?'

'It is December you know, and snowing.'

'We'll find some way to keep warm,' she laughed.

'If you think so, flipping heck, it will be time to get up at this rate, if we don't get a move on,' Tom joked. 'Leave the water in, I'll have a quick dip too, and I need a shave. Boy it's never this protracted in the movies.'

Jennifer came into the room wearing her dressing gown; she kissed and hugged Tom,

'I will only be a moment Jen, get the bed warmed,' and he went out. Jennifer was in the bed when he returned and she flicked the covers back. Tom stood for a moment, simply gazing at her, mirroring her smile. She reached up to him, and he lay down still looking into her eyes.

'Have I told you how beautiful you are, Jen?

'You are beautiful to me too, Tom.'

He took her gently into his arms, and smiled. 'Do you know Miss Dunwoody; I love you, really, really. It's quite frightening in a way. I love you so much.' Tom lowered his lips to hers and lightly ran his fingers down her side just touching the fine hair on her tummy, she sighed at the ecstasy. Her whole being was alive as never before. She was compelled to press her body to him. Her senses and emotions were all one, then they were one, they were man and wife at last, forever. This moment was eternal; no one could ever have been so in love as this, she was sure. This was/is heaven, she knew it as she cried out. There was "A completeness" now as they stilled, their two bodies, souls, and spirits, and they were one.

They lay wrapped in each other's arms. Tom kissed her again. Their lips parted and he held her with his cheek pressed against hers, his lips trembled and his voice betrayed his torment.

'I love you Jen there will never be anyone else, this is tough, you will wait for me to come to you, won't you, please?' Jennifer sensed his distress, she held him, stroking his hair, he was quiet, and she kissed his cheek. Gradually she felt him relax. He drew her firmly to his chest and kissed the top of her head, holding her as if, by his physical strength he could keep her here. 'I won't let you go, I simply can't. I don't know what to say about my feelings at this moment, Jen. It's just not fair, God, *please* don't do this to us, please, please, I'm begging, I will do anything, anything. Dear oh dear, I need to get a grip or I'm going to go flipping mad,' he said rubbing his face with his hand.

'Look Tom we don't know what's ahead, as I have said before, it's the same for everyone, but I do know I will be waiting for you. I don't know what it will be like, I just can't imagine, but I know all the love I have felt tonight will be there, waiting for you.'

'*I don't know*, we keep saying that. Somehow, it's not until life whacks you over the head with reality, that you realise that you actually flipping well "Don't know". At this minute, I have a master's degree, in "Don't know".'

'I do know it's nice to have someone to cuddle into, come on let's try to get some sleep, whether one likes it or not life goes on and you have to go to the gallery tomorrow.'

Chapter Eleven

Tom and Jennifer arrived late at the gallery the following morning.

'Morning, Ray,'

'Morning, Mr Jackson, morning Ma'am, cool out there.'

'Too right, let me introduce my fiancée, Lady Jennifer Dunwoody,' Jennifer offered her hand.

'Oh! Pleased to meet you, my Lady, by the way Mr Jackson, there is a gent over there wants a word, asked me to tell you when you came in.'

'Right, thanks Ray.' Tom and Jennifer went across to a smartly dressed man; Tom guessed he was in his fifties, the man turned to face them.

'Good morning, Sir, are you the artist?'

'Yes, Tom Jackson, this is my fiancée, Lady Jennifer Dunwoody, can I help you Sir?' Tom said, reaching out his hand.

'Pleased to meet you,' the man took Tom's hand and bowed his head, 'I'm Reginald Armstrong-Bennett, I represent the Weltzman institute in London, you may have heard of it?'

'Indeed I have Sir, it has quite a reputation in the art world.'

'I read about your exhibition in the Times and thought it worth a visit.'

'I'm pleased to meet you Sir, I hope you feel it has been worth your while, travelling up from London.'

'Very much so, I have been enthralled by your work. I have a proposition to make to you, is there anywhere we can talk in private?'

'I'm sure Ray, that's the caretaker, would allow us to use the office. If you follow me I'll ask him.'

'I'll wait here Tom,' Jennifer said.

'No you won't, you come too, you are my inspiration, together always, that's the deal, remember.' Tom asked the caretaker if they could use the office for a few moments and Tom showed Mr Armstrong-Bennett to a chair. Tom noticed that he flicked the chair with his gloves before he was seated. Tom imagined that this was not the usual sort of office, Mr Armstrong-Bennett was used to doing business in. He offered the remaining chair to Jennifer but she said she preferred to stand; Tom leant against the filing cabinet next to Jennifer and folded his arms, trying to appear as casual as he could.

'Now then Mr Armstrong-Bennett, what can I do for you?'

'Please call me Reginald, I'm afraid my names a bit of a mouthful, but it sounds impressive in my line of business.'

'Thank you, we're plain Tom and Jennifer, however having said that, that's not quite true. I was dragged from the gutter like a real artist, and my beautiful fiancée took pity on me, when she saw me begging on a bench by the sea,' Jennifer laughed and squeezed his hand.

The buyer laughed too, 'So Tom it is then. It's more what can I do for you Tom, but in truth it will be of benefit to us both. We would like you to exhibit in our gallery in London, then in New York.' Tom tried to look as if this was an everyday occurrence, Jennifer actually looked less surprised than he did. 'I would also like to purchase two of your paintings so that they would permanently belong to us. We would initially show one in our London gallery and the other in our New York gallery. I noticed that there are no prices shown for your work, they are for sale, I take it?'

'Yes, they are for sale, I determined I would let the public decide their worth. The intrinsic cost of a painting, overall, is not great, as you know. A little pigment, some canvas and a few hours work, but we both know that the prices are not set by adding up the cost of the constituent parts. People set the price, so I thought, let the people decide, thumbs up or down, death or life, that's my policy they the public, can make me any offer. I'm not saying that I will accept it, but it's a place to start.'

'Ah, an interesting idea, throw the ball into the buyer's court, very brave of you. You are a purist I can see; so many young artists think they are a gift to the art world. Alas I am compelled to concur with Francis Schaeffer, when he says, "Art has fallen below the line of despair", but great art is a constant and has an indefinable quality.'

'Painting is simple, that's why I have included some very basic representations. I love to see children's work. They are so uninhibited, it's something we lose as we become more "Sophisticated", fundamental, is difficult to achieve. Picasso managed it but it takes courage, one has to be able to face the taunts of, "Childish". How many times have I heard people say of Van Gogh, that their children could do better.'

'Ha, I understand, that's probably why I am drawn to your exhibits. The "Children" drawings, you even call them, "Children by the sea", I love the bright colours. The sky is blue, the sand is yellow, the houses are white, and the grass is green, straight from the tube, just as Vincent did. Let me simply say, "I love your work".'

'Thank you, I appreciate your kindness. Which two are you interested in?'

'Actually there are three, but I have been in this work for many years and I fancy, and I can't tell you why, that the portrait of your fiancée will not be for sale, it is quite remarkable. As I have said I am very excited by your work, never have I seen a portrait, which contained so much pathos. I have seen the benchmark for all portraits, in the Louvre in Paris, many times and to be quite honest, your portrait, of this dear Lady, moved me more. As you probably know the great man carried that portrait with him, wherever he went. I wonder if this portrait may have a similar future? Something about your work caused my eyes to fill with tears. I have never had that experience before in thirty-five years as a buyer and critic. That work alone will make you famous, Mr Jackson, Tom. My dear Lady, you are to marry a man of very rare talent.'

'I have told him that Sir; because painting is so effortless to him he underestimates his talent.' Tom was very much the third person in this conversation, he almost looked around to see who they were talking about.

'Quite, the two I would wish to purchase are called, "Swallows arrive in summer" and "Swallows leave in autumn". They could well be called, "Joy and Sorrow", for that's what they have managed to encapsulate. The emotion you have poured into those two pictures is breathtaking, but first, have they already gone?'

'No, not as yet, they are the two largest in the exhibition as you can see, and if you will forgive me, the two I am most proud of, they sum up a moment of my life.' The buyer glanced at Jennifer. 'I have had offers, which I am tempted by, but so far, I have decided against the sale. I think that you may understand Sir. For me, my work is not solely about making money. I paint because I can't help it. I have no plan, I merely paint, and therefore judging the merit of my own work is difficult. What one sees, is an expression of my view of the world in a moment of time.'

'I do understand, and believe me I recognise the value of these works. Let me ease the separation, I will put in the contract I have here, a buyback clause at the same price, if you ever wish to repurchase them. I ask also for an option to bid against any third party wishing to acquire the work in the future. That's a quick overview; it's our standard contract, or one of them, which I have brought with me. What do you say to that? I am prepared to offer ten thousand for the two. I realise that you may think that under valued.'

'Mmm, that seems fair – Jennifer.' Tom was sure in his effort to appear cool, his voice sounded as if he had been breathing hélium. Jennifer, who had previously been perfectly collected, now sat at Ray's table with all the grace and adroitness of an alcoholic, knocking a glass of water over in the process.

'Oops, Lady Jennifer, are you all right?' Mr Armstrong-Bennett said, catching the glass before it rolled off the table, fortunately there was only a little water in it.

'How do we proceed now, first, here is my card, Tom,' he passed it to him, along with the contract for Tom to consider. 'You may wish to consult your solicitor, but I assure you this is our standard practice. If you are happy would you sign it and if you would be so kind... Lady Jennifer, and witness it. I will arrange to have your work delivered to me. Will a cheque be satisfactory for payment for half the amount, to secure the works? It will take seven or so days to clear. Once you are satisfied with the contract, you can release the pictures to me and we will make the final payment. We have our own people who are specialists at transporting valuable art, they will see to it when you give me the word,'

'Yes,' Tom squeaked and coughed to clear his throat, as Mr Armstrong-Bennett took his chequebook from his inside pocket. He wrote the cheque and passed it to Tom.

'If you could furnish me with a contact address, I will be in touch.'

'Here's my card.' Fortunately, Tom had had some cards printed for this purpose, so that he would look as professional as possible. 'Actually, I, we, are between addresses at this moment, but if you send any correspondence to the address on my card, it will reach me.' Tom had given his sister's address. 'As soon as I have a more permanent address I will contact you, it should be within a couple of weeks.'

'I will give you a carbon copy from my book of sales and signed photographs of the work you have purchased.'

'Excellent, all very simple and straightforward, you seem very well organised.'

'Having to be organised, must be the one good thing I got from my time in hell, as a schoolteacher.'

'You were a schoolteacher! Teaching's loss is the art world's gain. Now then, I think that's everything, I will leave you and look forward to our next meeting.' With that, he stood, offered his hand and Tom showed him out. When Tom returned to the office he merely looked at Jennifer, they were both speechless, and then they laughed, and he hugged her, lifting her off the floor and spinning her around. Suddenly he stopped laughing, and set her down gently, he was quiet now, hugging her tightly he whispered as much to himself as Jennifer, 'Dear God, how can everything seem so perfect?'

'It's alright Tom this is good, all part of our life and I am happy, really I am, I never knew what it was to be happy, it is a completeness I could have only dreamt of. It's all part of it.'

'You must keep telling me, because I don't want to waste any time.'

'Tom, have your brothers and sister been to see your exhibition?'

'Sure, they came the first weekend.'

'What did they make of it?'

'I think they were astounded. They were all very generous, but they have always spoiled me, so I take their compliments with a pinch of salt. Come on I have had enough of families for now, I have something very particular to do before your mum and dad come this afternoon.'

'What?'

'Get your coat, it's a surprise.' Tom slipped on his coat then helped Jennifer on with hers. He led her by the hand into the town.

'But where are we going?' Then she realise as they neared the biggest jeweller's shop in the town. '*Tom!* I know where you are dragging me, and it's a waste of money, you don't have to do this.'

'Yes I do, don't be difficult woman.' Tom pushed Jennifer into the jeweller's and directed her to a cabinet with engagement rings displayed in it.

'Tom, everything in me says no, but they are beautiful, get behind me Satan.'

'This is what people do when they get engaged, that's us no difference, we are forever.' Jennifer reached up and kissed him. That must have signalled to an observant assistant that here was a possible sale.

'Sir, Madam, am I honoured to be witness to a singular event? I'm Mr Widsome, may I be of assistance?'

'Indeed, we wish to purchase an engagement ring, in the one thousand pound mark.' Jennifer actually gasped; the assistant lifted his eye to her and smiled.

'Tom! My car didn't cost that much.'

'Can I help it if you have a cheap car?' Jennifer kicked him.

'You are impossible.' The assistant clearly tried to ignore the interchange between Tom and Jennifer, but was unable to prevent a smile, 'I apologise Mr Winsome, but you must understand I am marrying a lunatic.'

'Ahhh, love makes fools of us all, Madam. Actually it's *Wid* – some, my dear lady.'

I don't want any details of your love life thank you very much, Tom thought, decidedly uneasy with the sales assistant's touchy feely approach to selling.

'Oh, I'm sorry, Mr Wid-some.'

'Think nothing of it, dear lady, a simple mistake, now perhaps Sir and Madam would care to view this tray?' He said, lifting a tray from behind a glass cabinet whilst treating them to his best ever so humble, creepy salesman's smile. 'Perhaps we could measure your finger so we can point you to your size. Though it is not really a problem if you prefer one of the others, resizing it is simple enough, we can attend to such an alteration on the premises.'

'Thank you,' said Tom leaning on the counter.

'My... Sir, what beautiful hands you have, you must be an artist.'

'What!' Tom quickly put his hands into his pocket and coughed.

Jennifer's uncertainty about Tom spending money, on what she considered an unnecessary expense, was overcome by the temptation of the sparkling light before her. She was determined to enjoy every second of this. She tried, this ring then that ring, and then the previous ring then the one before that. Eventually she decided on a ring with a pair of diamonds. They had been set in such a way that they appeared to be one.

'This is it Tom, it is perfect, symbolic, you and I, close together forever, I love it. Tom paid by cheque, as he made out the cheque, the fussy rather effeminate salesman reached over and squeezed Tom's hand, which was resting on the glass display case, saying, 'Good choice, Sir.' Jennifer could hardly contain her laughter at the look on Tom's face; it was bright red. Tom quickly stood, 'Shall I wrap the ring for madam?'

'No thank you, she will be wearing it.' Tom picked up the box, which belonged to the ring, took Jennifer by the elbow, and hurriedly directed her towards the door.

'Phew, let me get out of here, it's the last engagement ring I'm buying in that shop.'

Once outside Tom shivered, shook his shoulders, and relaxed. He was now able to focus on Jennifer again and he wasn't sure which sparkled the most, Jennifer's face, or the ring. They crossed the road, stopping briefly at a stand selling hotdogs to the Christmas shoppers. Tom paid the vendor, and they ate the hotdogs as they walked back to the gallery.

'Never let it be said that I don't know how to treat a lady, diamonds followed by a splash up meal to celebrate.'

'What more could a girl ask for.'

'It's all go, next your mum and dad, and I want to be at the gallery when they arrive, unless your pa has bottled out and decided against it.'

They dashed into the gallery, hoping her mother and father had not arrived whilst they were out.

'Quick give me your coat and ask Ray if we can steal some of his coffee, I am gasping for a cup.' It was a close run thing to know who was most nervous about Jennifer's mother and father's arrival; it was obvious that they were both trying to be calm. There was a good attendance for the last day and Tom sold two more pictures. He smiled, every time he looked at Jennifer she was admiring her ring, and he was pleased. It was while he was taking payment for a picture that they arrived. To everyone else they were simply more visitors, Jen went to them hugging her mother and kissing her father. He saw Jennifer through the office window, showing her ring to them, and was amused to watch their reactions. I had better go out and see them, said Tom to himself, thinking I have some sympathy for the poor fellow; I'll go to welcome them whilst I feel so amenable towards him. Tom gently eased his way past the visitors towards his future mother and father-in-law. Lady Carolyn smiled as she saw him coming towards them.

'Ah Tom, congratulations are in order,' said Jennifer's mother, her father made a token grunt, then her mother came to Tom and kissed him.

'Thank you for that, Lady Carolyn, I will do my very best for Jen, I want you to know that, she really is everything to me,' he whispered in her ear.

She stepped back from him; 'Do you know, I really think you will, Jennifer is glowing,' and she hugged him again. 'By the way where were you when I was getting an engagement ring,' and she smiled, Jennifer's father didn't look *quite* so amused.

Chapter Twelve

Actually, Tom thought, all things considered, it had gone fairly well with Jennifer's mum and dad.

'That's one hurdle over Jen, AND, it went better than I expected, you know what, I think your mum actually likes me.'

'How could she not?'

'Mmm, your father didn't seem to find me so irresistible.' Jennifer laughed and kissed him.

'So what now, Tom?'

'We will have to hang about and talk to the visitors; you can work your magic and extract as much cash as you can. You can be my chief salesman.' That's exactly what they did they sold three more pictures that afternoon. Jennifer showed a natural talent for talking to the visitors and making them feel welcome. This part was not really Tom's forte; he was an introvert and found it difficult to sell his work. He knew it was ridiculous, but it all seemed so pretentious. His basic instinct would have been to give his pictures away, but if he were going to make a living at this work, the future would be pretty bleak with such an approach. He was truly relieved to see that Jennifer was his other half in every sense, where he was hopeless, she excelled. By the time the doors closed, they were both exhausted.

'We can't do any more tonight Jen, I would have liked to get on with dismantling the exhibition, but Ray will want to go home, so there is nothing we can do until Monday.'

They said goodnight to Ray, the caretaker, and set off to return to the Red Lion where they were staying. It was snowing quite heavily now. Their travel was protracted because of the busy teatime traffic, made worse by the crowds of people leaving the football match.

'It's murder on match day; I wonder how the "Toon" went on today. They were playing Scunthorpe United.' Whilst they were waiting at some traffic lights, Tom rolled down the car window and asked a passer-by if he knew the score.

'Whey-man we slaughtered them, 3 – 1,' the happy man shouted back to Tom. Football was a large part of the town culture; the result of the team affected every aspect of town life.

'That's good news, Jen. Are you interested in football?'

'If you are Tom, so am I.'

'Get off with you.'

'The truth? It bores me to death.'

'Ha, that's more like it.'

'I know the "World Cup" is to be held here next, in 1966, and that's about the sum total of my knowledge, oh, and Brazil are the current holders, I read that too.'

'Very good, I'm impressed, most of my family, as small as it is, are avid supporters of the "Toon Army" as Newcastle are fondly known, but I'm not that bothered, I must be honest. I like to know they have won, but I wouldn't always know who they were playing.' They chatted on mindlessly as they wended their way to the Pub where they were staying. Tom knew he was nervous about the evening meal with Jennifer's mother and father, and he guessed Jennifer was too.

Eventually they pulled into the pub car park, the ground was covered with a scattering of snow, and it was bitter cold.

'Come on let's get into the warmth it's freezing out here Tom, the weather forecast is for a bad winter.'

'Who cares, I've got my love to keep me warm.'

'You are so corny, but cute,' Jen laughed.

Once in their room, Tom asked how she felt about their visit to her parents. 'What will be, will be, Tom.'

'What on earth will I wear, Jen, you have seen my wardrobe?'

'Just wear your evening suit, that will be fine.'

'WHAT!'

'Only joking.'

'You don't dress for dinner, please, you are kidding.'

'Of course I am, you watch to much, "Upstairs Downstairs", look Tom just be yourself your jeans will be fine.'

Tom made his best effort, but when he studied himself in the mirror, he thought it still looked as if he had dressed in the dark.

'Jen, I don't know how you do it but you always look fantastic to me,' he took her in his arms, then paused, looking at her, 'Gosh I have never noticed before, you have freckles.' She tried to wriggle away from his gaze.

'Oh, please, don't, I hate them; they make me look like, Anne of Green Gables, or Heidi. They generally make their appearance when I'm nervous, for some silly reason.'

'I love freckles.'

'Can we just leave it at that, and forget about them, please.'

'Certainly, Heidi, I mean Jen, let's go, once more into the breach dear friends and all that.'

'Tom!'

'Sorry Jen, slip of the tongue.'

'Mmm.'

Tom grabbed his coat and helped Jennifer with hers and they set off. She parked at the front of her parent's house; once again, the butler greeted them as they entered.

'Boy, my freckles must be showing now,' Tom joked, 'are you sure you know what you are doing getting engaged to a bum like me.'

'I'll give you a *kick* up the bum if you keep mentioning freckles. They will be in here.'

Jennifer opened the door and ushered Tom into the room. Her parents were sitting in much the same position, as they had been the night before. Her mother stood to greet them.

'Ah, Tom, Jennifer, come in and make yourselves comfortable,' Lady Carolyn said, smiling, Lord Peter stood too, and nodded. Jennifer and Tom sat very close together on an old leather settee. 'Dinner won't be too long, have you eaten much today?' Jennifer's mother asked.

'Not really Mummy, we have been very busy.'

'Have you a proper job as well as this painting thing, it's not a very secure future?' was Jennifer's father's offering by way of a greeting. Tom paused and took a deep breath, he was resolved not to rise to any provocation, for Jennifer's sake. He was determined to dig out every bit of gold their lives had to offer in the time they had together. He could see what he would have usually taken umbrage at, was a waste of their precious time.

'Actually, Sir, I have been offered the opportunity of an exhibition in London and New York.'

'Do you mind if I tell them what Mr Armstrong-Bennett offered, Tom.'

'I suppose not.'

'Tom sold two of his paintings for ten thousand pounds.'

'WHAT!'

'Mr Armstrong-Bennett, who has worked in the art world for years, works for a prestigious art gallery, the Weltzman institute in London.'

'What – *the* – Weltzman institute?' Her father blurted out.

'Yes, *the* Weltzman institute.'

On cue the butler came in, 'Dinner is served, my Lord,' Jennifer's father looked up.

'Ah, yes, thank you Warwick.'

'I hope that you like pheasant, Tom, it's that time of year.'

'To be honest Lady Carolyn, I have never had pheasant before, but I'm sure it will be fine. I'm not a faddy eater, mother insisted we clean our plates.' Actually, the meal was less formal than Tom had expected, even Jennifer's father was wearing jeans. Jennifer's mother was clearly at ease, the sort of person, like Jennifer he supposed, who was able to make everyone feel comfortable and welcome. She gave the impression of being totally relaxed with the person she was, it seemed she did not need to prove she was better than anyone else. They had wine with the meal; Tom thought it tasted dreadful, as dry as dust, but politely said he liked it, when asked by Jennifer's father if it was to his liking. Tom supposed that Lord Peter was making an effort to be, at the very least, polite.

Out of the blue Tom asked, 'Do you mind if I ask for some advice, Sir?' Jennifer pulled back her head and her mouth fell open. 'I have made a great deal of money, by my standards, I was wondering if you might advise me what best to do with it.' This completely caught out Jennifer's father.

'Ah, yes, well now.'

'I'm sure Peter will help you Tom, after all it's Jennifer's future too.'

Once Jennifer's father had assimilated Tom's approach for advice, Tom swiftly saw a completely different side to Lord Peter Dunwoody. Lord Peter was transformed, now friendly, and fully interested in the art world, almost passionate. He would introduce Tom to his associate who was a solicitor.

'Would tomorrow be convenient, Tom?' he asked.

'Actually tomorrow's Sunday, Sir.'

'Oh, that's not a problem, he will be only too pleased to help.'

'Is that okay with you Jen? We were going to church in the morning.'

'Church!'

'Yes, Daddy, church, you know that place with the pointy roof.'

'Mmm, tomorrow afternoon then, I'll organise it.'

'That's kind of you Sir, I really don't want to cause you any inconvenience.'

'No problem at all, as Carolyn says, this is Jennifer's future too.' Lord Peter actually got up from his meal to make the phone call and arrange the meeting. When he returned he confirmed the time at 2pm, he even insisted that Tom come for lunch after church. Tom was astounded at the change; suddenly he was very definitely the flavour of the month.

On their way home to the pub where they were staying, Jennifer remarked, that Tom had for sure pressed the right buttons with her father. 'To be fair Jennifer, I'm not too sure if I would have been much different in his position. You are his only daughter and he must have hoped for a better catch than "Yours truly".'

'Whatever, he seems alright now and that is a load off my mind, and probably Mother's too.'

'I am pleased he was so willing to be helpful. I have never had spare money to worry about before, so your father's help, is very much appreciated. I am going to have to get some new clothes, Jen. First thing Monday we will go to the Registrar office and find out what the score is, as far as a quick marriage goes. If we can pull it off before Christmas, that would be perfect. After that we will go shopping, and with your artistic fashion conscious eye of impeccable taste, you can help me choose some new clothes.'

'I must say it again, how non-stop exciting my life suddenly is,' Jennifer laughed.

'Mmm,' was the best Tom could manage, he felt that exciting, would not *quite* be the word he would choose. Turmoil may better fit the bill. For him, life at the moment seemed to be one nerve-racking experience after another.

'That was a turn up, you mentioning church like that, Tom, that must be what's called thinking on your feet, it wrong footed daddy.'

'I thought we needed to claw back some ground. I felt your dad was weighing up our relationship in his mind, and on balance, the scale was tipping towards the mortal sinner side. With our new-found wealth *and* a trip to church, it might have levelled out. You don't think, I over did it, do you?'

'Ha, it caught me out for sure, anyway, we'll have to go through with it now.'

'At least you know what a church looks like, apparently they have pointy roofs, that's way ahead of what I know about church. Anyway in for a penny in for a pound.'

Tom was decidedly uneasy about their trip to Church, however, the people there seemed very welcoming to the young couple. Some already knew Jennifer, even though it had been a while since she had been there. The people made an effort to come and talk to them. When Tom turned around, he realised Jennifer had left him, after a moment's panic, he spotted her talking to an elderly lady and he made his way quickly to join her. Jennifer introduced Tom; the lady was pleased to tell him she had known Lady Jennifer since she was a "Bairn" and was equally pleased to see she had found herself such a fine young man. Others had actually been to Tom's exhibition and seemed honoured to have him at their church. He struggled to imagine how they saw him. He didn't feel any different from them, it was he, who felt awkward and shy, but because of his particular "God given" gift, they thought he was unique in some way. It was a relief to sit down and assumed a prayerful kneeling position. He was only copying what everyone else seemed to be doing and Jennifer knelt by him. He closed his eyes just enough to be able to look prayerful and yet keep an eye on what was happening. People appeared to kneel for a few moments, then sit back, so he did likewise. He was unsettled for a moment because Jennifer continued to kneel after he had risen from his knees and assumed his seat again. He wished now he had watched her instead of the lady in the pew in front of him. He was in a dilemma, perhaps he had not knelt long enough, then thankfully as he was about to kneel again, Jennifer sat back, smiling and took his hand. He should have taken more time to prepare for this. He didn't think it was going to be so complex. Jennifer seemed perfectly at ease; he hadn't a clue which page of the book they were on, as soon as he found the page they turned over to a different place in the book. Why didn't it follow one page after another? Who the flipping heck designed this layout? He wondered. Tom couldn't concentrate on a word that was being said, he was so confused by the mechanics of the service. Everyone seemed to know instinctively when to stand or sit, he felt that it was like doing the hokey cokey, he wasn't any good at that either. He was beginning to sweat, he ran his finger around his shirt collar, he hadn't worn a tie since he packed in teaching and his collar was getting tighter by the second. Next, the sermon and a moment's rest, he hoped, and some time to regroup his senses. That was after the kafuffle of him sitting, whilst everyone else stood, until the vicar chappie climbed into the pulpit, Tom quickly stood just as everyone else sat. He felt to be seconds out of sync with the rest of the congregation; he was putting his left-foot in when everyone else it appeared was putting their left-foot out, for sure he was shaking all about, 'What a flipping nightmare,' he said under his breath. Jen smiled again, and he tried to return her smile as if he was perfectly relaxed. It was all gobbledygook, he couldn't make sense of a word the fellow said, and his brain was running on overload. Then the preacher said something about, all God wanted, was us – him – Tom Jackson – to know that He loved him. He kept saying, 'Do you know that I love you?' That was all Tom could hear and he was mesmerised by the words, 'Do you know that I love you?' Eventually, it was all over and he was walking out and shaking hands with the vicar at the door.

'What a nice man, do you know what Tom, I really enjoyed the service, and you coped very well.'

'Jen I can honestly say, I don't know what to say,' she laughed and leant into him.

'Do you know that God loves you Jen?'

'That's the line, do I know – I never really thought about it, I must be honest. One thing I do know – I love you Mr Jackson. Come on lunch now, then on to the next meeting, I will have to get a bigger diary at this rate.'

'You will come with me when I go with your dad to see his business chap?'

'If you want me to.'

After lunch, Tom's now best friend, Lord Peter, took them to visit his friend, Finnley Henderson, of Henderson & Henderson, at his home. This was a whole new world for Tom, none of this, we'll try to fit you in, two weeks, on Wednesday, to keep the hoi polloi in their place, no way, will *now* be soon enough, Tom smiled as they drove. Jen had offered to sit in the back; he wasn't up to incidental chatter with his Lordship. They pulled onto the gravelled drive, which crunched and crackled opulence as they drove up to the front door. His Lordship only knocked once and walked in. Mrs Henderson, of Henderson & Henderson, Tom assumed, came to greet them, and kissed both Jennifer and her father.

'Lovely to see you Jennifer, gosh, Jeremy will be disappointed to have missed you; I know how fond you are of him. He's busy at the moment setting up some new venture, import export thing, with some people in

Rhodesia, he's frightfully clever, isn't he, Peter.'

'Yes, he's a bit of a whiz, and he's been kind enough to give me a piece of it, fine fellow.'

'You'd never believe it Jennifer, Jeremy was attacked by some young hoodlums, just the other day; they beat him viciously and broke his nose. He fought valiantly as you can imagine, but there were too many of them, they left him for dead. He is in a dreadful mess, my poor boy, we had to rush him to hospital, for all the use they were.' Jennifer looked at Tom but it didn't seem to be registering.

'Dreadful, dreadful, I'd flog the lot of them, the law's too soft by far,' said Lord Peter.

'Anyway, no doubt you will be desperate to see him but it will have to be another day, you've come to see Finnley, he said that you were popping around. He's in the garden, the water in the pond is frozen solid, and he's worried about his prize carp. I'll give him a shout, just find a chair in the drawing room, he won't be a moment.'

'May I introduce my fiancé, Daphne?' Asked Jennifer, 'this is Tom,'

'The artist, you see I know all about you, how thrilling to be famous. You will make Jeremy terribly jealous, I had great hopes for you two.' She said, turning to Jennifer. Oh, how jolly, jolly, Tom thought, but only nodded and took her offered hand. 'Would you like some tea whilst you chat, Peter.'

'No, not for me, we have only just finished luncheon, thank you.' They sat down, Tom took Jennifer's hand; Tom was well out of his comfort zone here. It was only a couple of minutes before Mr Henderson joined them.

'Ah, Peter, Jennifer, I assume this is Mr Jackson, the esteemed artist.' No I'm not, I've only had one exhibition and struck lucky, creep, Tom thought. These people are way too nice, nice for me, all polished and smooth. It's probably only skin deep, I will never fit in here, not if I live to be a thousand, which I hope I don't. He cast a sad glance at Jennifer.

Tom managed to collect himself long enough to ask Mr Henderson to read the contract that Mr Armstrong-Bennett had given him.

'Do you wish me to deal with this, Tom?'

'Err, yes, I had never really thought about it.'

'Not a problem.' It appeared that all Tom needed to do was give his obliging solicitor his bank details and that would be that. He signed one or two bits of paper, and Bob's your uncle they were travelling back to his Lordship's castle.

When they stepped out of the car, Tom quickly caught Jennifer's hand and drew her near enough to whisper, 'Jen, can we go into town, perhaps to the pictures. I need to be alone with you, my head is spinning?'

'Sure, that would be fun, they are showing Charade, with Audrey Hepburn and Cary Grant at the Odeon, I fancy seeing that. I'll just tell mummy where we are going.' They said their goodbyes, 'We will call tomorrow evening, Mummy, and let you know the outcome from our meeting with the Registrar, and then we'll arrange with you when it is convenient to move into the Lodge.'

'Really, you can move in more or less straight away, Darling, it will only need a bit of a spruce up, I will attend to that, and I will see that there is fresh linen and towels.'

'Thank you Mummy, that is ever so kind. Tom and I will be busy at the art gallery in the afternoon, clearing away. Oh, and Mummy, there's one other thing, Tom will need to store his work somewhere for the time being, before it's taken to London, do you mind if we have it brought to the Lodge?'

'Not at all, that will be perfectly alright, won't it Peter?'

'Mmm.'

'You won't over do it Jennifer?' her mother asked.

'No, she will be consigned to tea making duty, Lady Carolyn,' Tom quickly jumped in.

'I'm sure you will look after her Tom, we will see you when we see you.'

Chapter Thirteen

Tom was glad to be alone with Jennifer; they ate out in the town. Over the meal, Jennifer quizzed Tom about how he felt the meeting went with her father's associate.

'I don't know really,' he replied, 'they are people from another planet. I remember a story my dad used to tell about two farmers arguing over who owned a cow. One was pulling on the head the other was pulling on the tail whilst the lawyer was underneath milking it.' Jennifer laughed. 'All a touch too smooth for my taste, yes sir, no sir, ever so humble, sir. Fortunately we were spared the amazing Jeremy, an old flame of yours by the sound of it.'

'You very definitely jest; he is the most arrogant self-opinionated, slime-ball you could possibly imagine and a male chauvinist to boot. I apologise for the Americanism, but it fits the bill perfectly'

'Oh, so you like him then?' Tom laughed.

'You've met him.'

'*I have?*'

'Yes, outside the pub the night we met.'

'Ahhh... *that* was the amazing Jeremy, I remember now, a charming affable chap, nice cravat?'

'AND... on your last meeting, you broke his nose.'

'Ohhh, *that* Jeremy, ah, I didn't *connect*, stupid or what. The description of his brave defence against the wild rampaging proletariat hoards misled me.'

'Apparently, you did *connect* with his nose, by all accounts. Yes, that was him, I don't know why Father bothers with him, he is truly obnoxious.'

'I'm probably off his Christmas card list now.'

'I would rather we forget about him completely Tom. Come on let's eat drink and be merry...' Jennifer stopped short on the flippant quote and Tom never commented.

The restaurant where they decided to go was quite near the cinema, which meant they were able to walk to it.

They talked more than watched the screen. So much so, a rather disgruntled man in the row behind them tapped Tom on the shoulder, 'Look, if you wants to watch the picture, watch it, if you wants to talk, go somewhere else, so the rest of us who've paid good money to watch it, can watch it.' They apologised profusely. When Tom did focused on the movie, he really had no idea what was happening he obviously hadn't concentrated on a single scene. He wanted to ask Jennifer, but thought better of it, afraid of incurring another rebuke. When he glanced at her, she gave him a look, which said, she was as lost as he was. She glanced again at him, stifled a giggle, tugged his hand, and flicked her head suggesting that they may as well go. Tom nodded and they decided to leave, unfortunately, that caused further disruption, as people in their row were compelled to stand to let them pass.

'Boy, I bet they're glad to see the back of us.' Tom said, as he held the cinema door for Jennifer and they stepped out into the cold night air. 'Burr, it's freezing, Jen. Going to the pictures was not one of my better ideas, sorry to spoil it for you,' Tom said as they walked back to the car.

'Ha, don't bother, all I want, is to be alone with you. I don't care what we do so don't fret. I don't know about you but I have never been in love before, I have had boyfriends and crushes, I suppose, but nothing like this. Whey-man, this is serious stuff,' Jennifer attempted a Newcastle accent, 'you have cast your wicked spell on me,' she walked ahead of him, turned and waved her hands as if she was casting a spell.

'Ha, I thought it was me, under your spell, I submit, it's the best. I wake and you are there, my first thought, mad eh?' He reached out and took her hand and she again walked by his side. 'It was the worst moment ever; when you told me you were leaving, that day on the beach. I woke up every morning and you were on my mind, the thought that I would never see you again was unbearable.'

'I'm sorry for that Tom. I caused us both unnecessary suffering, and wasted precious time together. I still think this is selfish of me. However, as you say, it is all a kind of madness, and I thank God for it. Funny how He keeps popping up, somehow what I feel, and God seem inexorably linked.'

They were first down for breakfast the next morning. While they were eating, Tom asked what was the next step with her treatment. She put her cup carefully down and looked pensive, 'I have an appointment with Mrs Hart, my consultant, on the 17th of this month.'

'Jennifer, I need to know these things; unpleasant as it is to think about, it's part of our life, and that's all there is to it. Will that involve more debilitating treatment?'

'Honestly, I don't know.'

'You will be my wife next time you go, come on let's get off to sort out our wedding.'

Jennifer was silent for a while as they travelled; Tom guessed she was thinking about the trip to the doctors, now he had brought it up. He squeezed her shoulder as she drove; she leant her head and pressed her cheek against his hand. 'Tom, it is so wonderful to have you in my life, this would have been impossible without you.'

'Get off, I'm the lucky one, everyone looks at me, and I know they are asking, "Who's that lucky guy?", then to cap it all I get to sleep with this fantastic woman, now how good is that?' She smiled and cuffed a tear from her cheek.

It appeared that getting married was simple; the earliest would be Monday, two days before Christmas.

'Wow, perfect, we will be officially man and wife on Christmas Day.' Tom said smiling and hugging Jennifer, then with a look of concern he said, 'Unfortunately, that will mean we won't be married when you go to see the doctor.'

'You will still come with me, Tom?'

'Of course, if it will be alright.'

'Yes, I want you there, Mother came before but I need you now.'

They spent the afternoon at the Gallery. Tom was a little shocked when he calculated the commission the gallery was taking.

'Wow, the only thing free in this world is the cheese in the trap.' He took out his chequebook to pay the manager who had turned up, but Jennifer laid her hand on his arm.

'Listen Tom, for once, let me pay this, just in case your banking isn't sorted out yet and your cheque bounces, you don't want to start out with black marks against your name.'

'What! Your dad will have kittens.'

'He won't know.'

'I'm not sure about this.'

'I am and that's it.' Jennifer paid the bill, but Tom still wasn't happy.

'Jen, all my life others have picked up the tab for me, and it's still happening, sorry to seem so ungrateful. You are right of course but it makes me feel pretty shabby.'

'Forget about it, I will take it out on your body later,' he tried to smile.

When they returned to Jennifer's house with the news and dates, Tom was sweating, he was sure Jennifer's father would know that Jennifer had paid his bill, it would be written all over his face. As it happened, they were more anxious about the time-frame of the wedding. His Lordship was more than a little concerned what people would think of this unseemly haste to marry. Both, Tom and Jennifer ignored his concerns.

'I have had the Lodge cleaned today Jennifer, so you can move in whenever it suits you,' her mother informed them. 'Tomorrow we can go and look for a wedding dress, I have spoken to Stanley and he will take the horsebox to the gallery, and wherever you need it Tom, to collect your belongings.'

'You are a star, Mummy.'

'Thank you Lady Carolyn, I was going to organise a van to pick up my stuff, this saves me the trouble, if you're sure it's okay.'

'Certainly.'

'If you don't mind Mummy, we will go, and return first thing tomorrow. Have you a key for the Lodge handy so I can show Tom on the way out?'

It was only a couple of hundred yards to the Lodge at the gate. Jennifer opened the door with a sharp shove. 'This is an excellent start; makes me feel at home when the door's stiff,' they both laughed.

'Wow, this is very commodious. We must get a Christmas tree. It is nice and warm; your mum must have had the fires lit. Come on let's get off, it's still trying to snow.'

The following day, his Lordship was nowhere to be seen. Tom feared he would be assisting, him collect his work. How dumb, of course he wouldn't, he's probably never done a day's physical work in his life, Tom thought, smiling at his stupidity.

Jen kissed Tom as she left with her mother, 'It will be strange without you Tom, I promise we will be as quick as we can.'

'You enjoy this time with your mother, I would imagine buying your wedding dress with your mum is a very special deal.'

'That is kind of you Tom, I appreciate you saying that,' her mother said, clearly touched by Tom's consideration.

Tom met Stanley with the horsebox and they hit it off straight away. What a pleasant bloke Tom thought, more my sort of guy, not like that smarmy Mr Henderson, of Henderson & flipping Henderson.

It was nearly 6pm when Jennifer walked into the Lodge, flopping down onto Tom's knee, and kissing him, as he sat in an armchair by a roaring fire.

'This is perfect, I love you, and *our* home.'

'Have you had a good day playing, whilst I have been grafting?'

'Cheek, buying wedding dresses is hard graft too, I will have you know, Mr Jackson.'

'Was it successful?'

'It was wonderful.'

Chapter Fourteen

'This is never ending, Jennifer. I'm going to have to take you to meet *my* family now, and I can tell you I am as nervous about that as I was about meeting *your* mum and dad.'

'What have you to worry about, it's me who will be under inspection, what if they don't like me?'

'You don't have to worry about that, of course they'll like you, just give them one of your smiles. It's introducing them to Lady Jennifer Dunwoody, that makes me nervous, I'm a flipping wreck just saying the words.'

'Don't say it then. I hope I will be plain *Jennifer* to them. Anyway, it's Lady Jennifer, *Margaret*, Dunwoody.'

'You're joking me?'

'Nope, don't you like my name?'

'It's not that, actually I like the name *Margaret*, my mum was called Margaret, and I loved her too. No, it's just that there is a surprise at every turn. I will have to tell them you are a Lady. I don't want them dropped in it, and made to look foolish.'

'Tom, you worry too much.'

'Okay, but what they will think about their kid brother marrying into royalty, I can't imagine.'

Jennifer laughed, 'Hardly royalty, daddy's merely a minor northern Lord whose grandfather bought a title, more or less, no great shakes.'

'That's from where you are standing. Your dad is in effect their boss, he's one of the shareholders of the shipyard, I have gleaned that much. Anyway, we will go to our Molly's house first, you will like Molly. I will ring her, she has a phone, and *bay windows*.' Tom smiled as he recalled the expression on Molly's face, when she told him that the house they were buying had *bay windows*. Very upmarket, bless her cotton socks. 'I'll ask her to gather my clan at her house, we'll go after we have had some tea, if she's in, that is.'

Tom rang Molly and said he had some great news to share with them all, asking her to give Fred and Michael a shout. Molly said that she would do that. She asked him if he'd stay for supper, and he said he didn't want her to go to any trouble, but he'd love to if that were all right. It had been a while since he'd seen them all. Tom added that he was bringing a lady to meet them.

Tom smiled as he related the conversation to Jennifer because he knew Molly would be driven mad with curiosity.

Jennifer's mother had called at the Lodge with a ham quiche that saved them having to make a meal, which worked into their plans perfectly. They told her that they were going to meet Tom's family that night. Carolyn smiled and related to them *her* recollections and fears when going to meet Peter's family "Officially", for the first time. She told them she had met them before on holiday, but remembered the feeling well and how terrified she had been as they turned onto the drive, a mere farmer's daughter, to meet Lord and Lady Dunwoody.

'Your grandfather, Lord John, was an M.P. at the time and I was even younger than you are now, I was only twenty. It will all work out darling don't worry.'

'Thank you Mummy your kind words have managed to make me even more nervous,' Jennifer said.

Jennifer drove to where Molly lived, Tom talked all the way, hoping to distract her, or was it to help alleviate his own nerves he wasn't sure.

As they approached the house, Tom said, 'Turn left here, this is the drive up to her house, not unlike yours really, but we call it a street.' Jennifer laughed. 'This is posh here compared to where I used to live, believe me. Never the less, it would be best to park under that street lamp. Molly's house is there.' Tom pointed to a 1940s semi-detached.

'I am awfully nervous, Tom. I keep saying in my head that they are your brothers and sister so they must be like you.'

'Ah, I suppose they must, come on you will be fine. They won't be "Awfully" nervous I know that much, but they might be "Flipping" nervous.'

'I'm sorry what do you mean?'

'Come on you lump, I'm only teasing you.'

Jennifer held Tom's hand tightly as they walked across the road and up the short path to the front door.' Tom rattled the knocker a couple of times and Jim, Molly's husband came to the door.

'Now then, what fettle the day bonny lad, long time no see, come in come in, hello Miss.'

'Hello,' Jennifer replied. Oh, heck thought Tom, his stress levels hitting clinical neuroses. Jen's only spoken one word and all I can hear is posh, nightmare, how can you make "Hello" sound posh?'

Jim showed them into the front room. They were all there, even his niece Peggy, this is "In at the deep-end", perhaps this wasn't such a brilliant idea Tom thought, suddenly feeling hot under the collar. They all stood and smiled, hello, hello, hello echoed around the room, Molly came and hugged Tom, and smiled at Jennifer.

'This is my fiancée, Jennifer, thought I would let you know I'm getting married, before Christmas actually. Don't give me that look, Molly, it's nothing like that.'

'I never said a word.' They all smiled and shook hands with Jennifer.'

'Howay, pull up a chair, pet, make yasel' comfy,' Jim said.

'Would you like a cup of tea?' asked Molly.

'Thank you that would be jolly nice.'

'Hang about Molly, yes, tea would be good, but I have got to get this out in the open so I can begin to feel normal and relax.'

'Howay, then spit it oot,' Fred encouraged.

'Jennifer is actually Lady Jennifer Dunwoody. It's no big deal, we are just two people in love and Jen is going to be one of the family, for heaven's sake she likes me, shows how ordinary she is.'

'Don't worry lass, we won't look down on ya 'cause you're just a Lady,' said Fred, they all laughed, even Jennifer. Tom tried but he was too stressed at that moment.

'Was that all it was Tom? Right I'll get the tea, don't say anything till I get back, I don't want to miss anything.' Molly went out to the kitchen, leaving Tom with a totally vacant expression on his face. Okay, right, that was no big deal then, he thought to himself.

'You're not related to one of the big gaffers at the shipyard, Lady Jennifer, we hev a Lord Peter Dunwoody on the board if I'm no' mistaken?' asked Fred.

'Yes I am, he's my father, and I will get him to sack you if you continue to call me

Lady Jennifer,' she smiled and Fred laughed. 'Tom always calls me Jen, when I'm in his "Good-books" anyway, and I actually prefer that.'

'Good on ya lass, Jen it is then,' said Michael. 'I think that some praise is due too... Jen, I have never seen wor Tom looking so smart,' they all laughed. 'He usually looks as if he got dressed by accident.'

'What a cheek, I have always been a trend setter.'

'Thankfully, it's a trend that has never caught on,' Michael said ruffling Tom's hair.

'You see what you have "*Not*" missed being an only one, Jen,' Tom said.

'I think you are very fortunate, Tom.'

'As I suspected, you are quite mad,' he responded squeezing her hand and smiling.'

'Are you really a Lady?' asked Peggy shyly hugging into her mother.

'I try to be, but I'm not awfully good at it. Your Uncle Tom tells me you are a lady too and I have a favour to ask of you.'

'What is it, Lady?'

'I would rather you called me Aunty Jennifer or Jen if you prefer.'

'Aunty Jen?'

'Yes, because I am going to be your Aunty, you will have three Aunts then. Your Uncle Tom and I are to be married and I would like you to be my bridesmaid, would you do that for us, we would be honoured if you would?'

'Can I, Mummy?'

'Of course you can.'

'Will I have a posh frock?'

'Most certainly, you can come with your mummy and I, and choose the one you like.' Peggy was all smiles now and her mother squeezed her.

'Here's Molly. That was quick lass, ya've missed nowt, diven't fret.' Molly set the tray of food on a coffee table, which her husband Jim had moved into the centre of the room for the very purpose. Molly, clearly, had baked for the occasion; the tray was piled high with food.

'If this is the standard I am aiming for Molly, Tom is going to be seriously disappointed,' Jennifer commented nodding towards the cakes, Molly beamed. They were all obviously happy and wanted to be told every detail of how Tom and Jennifer had met. Then they each in turn told stories about Tom, some he'd never heard and some he wished had been forgotten. They also asked how the exhibition had gone and Tom told them about Reginald and the proposed exhibitions in London and New York.

'So we ha' somebody famous in the family, what dee yee think aboot that Maureen, pet.'

'When will all this happen Tom?' Maureen asked.

'Not until after Christmas now, Maureen, we have the wedding to sort out first.'

Fred told Tom he had been to the Weltzman Institute when he was sent to London to buy some equipment for the shipyard. He'd had some free time and loved to go to the art galleries whenever he could. Tom was stunned; he suddenly felt that he had never known his brother, fancy all this time Fred had been interested in art and I never knew, but then he thought, "Why should I be, Fred is my brother".

'I never knew you were interested in art Fred. Have you ever painted?'

'Aye, a dabble a bit ya knaas, I sketch more.'

'Well I never, I can't believe that I have never seen anything you have done.'

'Whey, you wor the artist, I'd have been embarrassed, tee show ye.'

'That's absurd and I'm ashamed that I never knew.'

'Whey man they're no worth yor time.'

'Yes they are, don't make me feel worst than I already do.'

Jennifer in her inimitable fashion got them all talking and telling their stories. By the time they had eaten Molly's cakes they were all relaxed and laughing. Tom felt he had learnt more about his family this evening, than he had ever known.

When Tom and Jennifer left they all hugged and kissed her, apart from Peggy, who had fallen asleep on the knee of her future aunt and was taken upstairs to sleep on her Aunty Molly's bed. It hadn't taken Jennifer long to work her magic on Peggy.

Ever present was the reality of their lives and Jennifer's health. This was a constant cloud always threatening to overwhelm Tom. The worst moment for him was when he saw Jennifer, cuddling Peggy who had fallen asleep on her knee. He couldn't speak and sat quietly for some time forcing a smile; afraid that his family might notice his misery and ask questions, which he didn't want to answer. He knew Jennifer wanted them to *live* each day, and not allow her health to overwhelm their daily lives. Most of the time, he managed fairly well, but then there were the moments such as the one, which he had just experienced, when he saw Jennifer holding his niece.

'Well, I never,' Tom said smiling, as they walked to Jennifer's car, 'it's still here, this is your lucky night.'

'Do you know, Tom, I can't remember when I had such a pleasant evening. Your family are wonderful and just like you.'

'Really, in what way.'

'They laugh and make life a fun place to be, I loved them.'

'They seemed to love you, *do you* know, you bring life to people, I can't remember ever seeing them all so animated. And, I know something else.'

'What?'

'I'm in love with an angel.'

'You're not in love with *me* then.'

'Come on woman, home.'

Chapter Fifteen

'It's the postman Tom, I'll get it.'
'What is it?'
'The most important letter is your provisional driving licence.'
'Mmm, that didn't take too long, we will have to look at organizing some driving lessons after Christmas.'
'No we won't, we will go up to your house today, it's only an hour or so easy driving to get to it, and you have not been there since you left to come to Newcastle for the exhibition. From there it is only fifteen minutes to the old aerodrome where you can practice.'
'Oh, heck, I suppose I should go to the house, but, err, well... I left it in a bit of a mess.'
'What do you mean, it was always a mess?'
'Cheek! No, you see, you had left me and I was at a very low point, Jen you have no idea.

I thought I was going mad.' Tom sat leaning on his knees looking at the floor.

'You think I don't know!'

'If you felt as bad as me, I'm sorry.'

'You have nothing to be sorry about, Tom. It was my fault and I know deep down that I should have stuck to my guns, but I'm glad I'm pathetically weak,' Jennifer turned and looked out the window.

'Aye, me too,' and Tom stood up and went to her, taking her in his arms.

'We're still going to go and do this today, Tom,' Jennifer said, after she had regained her composure. 'I will help you to clean up your house. I know I will need you to be able to drive as time goes on.'

'Yes... I suppose so.'

Jennifer parked her car outside the house Tom rented. She glanced at the sea; it wasn't so welcoming as the last time she had been here. There was a strong northeast wind blowing and the waves were crashing up the beach. There was still a beauty, perhaps it was the wild untameable respect demanded by nature, which drew her.

'I never thought I would be parking outside this door ever again, it's a weird feeling,' she shouted, hanging onto her car door as she climbed out, for fear it was ripped off by the wind.

'You might not think it such a great event when you see inside,' he called back to her. Tom's first challenge, as usual was his front door, it was tighter than ever what with the damp weather and not having been opened for a few weeks. Once opened, they were met with the toxic fumes of oil paint, which had been distilling in the sealed environment whilst he had been away.

'Phew, open the windows and the back door Tom before I pass out. How on earth did you live in this mess.'

'It wasn't *quite* as bad as this when I was here, *not quite*, and of course most of the canvases have gone to Newcastle.'

'What about all these in your bedroom, priceless artworks looking as if they are bound for the tip, not, the walls of the rich and famous.'

'Ah, there are those few.'

'*A few*, Tom! There must be fifty canvases. There are more under the bed.'

'So there are, well spotted Jen. I'll sweep the floor and stack them neatly in the other room where I paint.'

The windows and the back door were every bit as difficult to open as the front door.

'Light the fire Tom, it will dry the place while we work, it is very damp. It's not fit for human habitation. That's the first job, where to turn next is not quite so clear.'

'I did tell you Jen.'

Every room was a shambles, his bed was unmade, and the sheets were filthy. There was decaying food left out in the kitchen and the sink was full of dirty pots and pans.

'Tom, I'm so sorry I left you like this, I can't believe you were living in here.'

'Forget it, that's past, cleaning is symbolic of a new start. I have some plastic bags in the woodshed at the back of the cottage; my logs for the fire were delivered in them. All of the things we are going to throw out stack in a pile in the middle of the floor. I'll put them in the bags and leave it outside for the refuge men. I'll pop down to Charley at the pub and ask him to see that they take it away. That includes the bedding. They worked tirelessly for three hours, and eventually it was looking habitable.

'Gosh, Tom I'm filthy, my hair is like wire, I've broken two fingernails *and* I can feel the dust in my mouth, *and* I don't think I'll ever get rid of the frightful smell of paint.'

'Not a problem, I'll get my tin bath down and you can have a quick scrub up in front of the fire,'

'You jest, I would rather suffer until we get home, thank you all the same.' Tom laughed.

'Right,' he said, 'we have done enough. Jen, you look shot, come on let's catch a quick bite at the pub and get back home.'

'You are a shocker, Tom Jackson, the food and drink's a good idea, especially the drink, I'm gasping, but we are not going home until you have practised in the car.'

'Oh, yes the car, slipped my mind.'

'Hmm, of course it did,' Jen said stabbing him in the ribs with her elbow.

It was raining lightly, but thankfully not icy, when they arrived at the old aerodrome. Jennifer knew that the conditions were not perfect for someone who had never driven a car before but they could have been worse, and their lives seemed forever determined by the constraints of time. Tom jumped out of the car to open the gate onto the airfield, and Jennifer drove through onto the wide runway, stopped the car, switched off the engine, and climbed out.

'Okay, this is it, Tom, you get into the driver's seat and adjust it so you feel comfortable, there is a lever there,' she pointed to the lever, to slide the seat back and forward. 'Try pressing the pedals, make sure your legs are not fully extended when the pedals are pressed to the floor.'

'Yes, yes, I'm not *totally* stupid you know.' Jennifer paused and glared at him through the open door, then she walked around the front of the car, Tom got out, and she slid into the passenger seat. She was suddenly beginning to have doubts about the wisdom of *her* teaching Tom to drive.

Jennifer narrowed her eyes and looked at him as he climbed behind the steering wheel and adjusted his seating position. I'm catching a glimpse of a side to Tom Jackson that has its roots in a primeval past, where men are under some delusion that they are superior to women, she thought to herself.

'Ha,' she said.

'Pardon?' Tom asked, looking at her.

'Nothing darling, just some foolish misapprehension, I must deal with.' Settling into the passenger seat Jennifer went through the basics, explaining the gears and the function of the individual foot peddles. 'Now, make sure it's out of gear, turn on the engine, depress the clutch, put it into gear, release the handbrake and *gently* ease up the clutch. You will feel the gears start to engage, at the same time carefully press down on the accelerator.'

'Right, got that, pretty straight forward.'

'I will *repeat* that, as you release the clutch, you press the accelerator, left foot up, right foot down, have you got that?'

'Yes, it's not exactly rocket science, even women drive.'

'Ohhh, Tom, it's not a motor accident you need to worry about, this is a very lonely place it would take days to find a body here.'

'Ho, ho, ho, very droll.'

'Right, let's go, do as I...' Brummmm... the engine screamed, Bump, bump, bump, this was the kangaroo start of all kangaroo starts, the car jerked and bounced forward, 'TOM! NOT SO FAST.' Tom panicked; they were heading off the runway onto the grass and lurching towards a wartime air raid shelter. 'BRAKE TOM, TOM PUT YOUR FOOT ON THE BRAKE,' Jennifer shrieked, Tom was frozen solid; Jen pushed the gear stick, into neutral, the engine roared. They glided slowly to a stop, aided by the resistance from the long grass. Jennifer sat silently, slowly releasing her breath, the engine noise was deafening. Tom's foot eventually relaxed and the screaming engine stilled. Her heart was pounding against her ribcage; they both merely stared in horror at the concrete structure about six-foot before them. Tom was still clinging to the steering wheel his knuckles were white; there were beads of sweat on his forehead. After several minutes Jennifer swallowed and said, as calmly as she was able, 'Okay, you get out,' her voice trembled. She had to repeat herself before Tom reacted, 'Tom, let go of the steering wheel and get out. I'll reverse the car back onto the WIDE runway and we'll try again.'

As she stepped out of the car, she realised her legs were shaking and had to steady herself by leaning against the car roof, before she could walk around to the driver's seat. Tom slowly got out of the car, very sheepishly, avoiding any eye contact with her as they passed by each other. Jennifer slid onto the seat, resting her forehead on the steering wheel for a moment, and then reversed the car well clear of the air raid shelter. She was still shaking when they changed places.

'Now, Tom shall we attempt starting the car and moving off once more? Try to forget that this is a runway designed for aircraft, we are not trying to get *airborne*.' There was a more humble Tom now, as he sat once again at the wheel of the car, he did not have any clever rejoinder this time. He took Jennifer's sarcasm without a murmur.

However, after two hours, they had recovered from the initial thrills of "First flight", Jennifer had relaxed and they were on speaking terms again. She even felt confident enough to allow Tom to drive the five or six miles on the country lanes to the main road. She only had to point out twice, that motorists usually drive on the left, in England anyway.

They both knew that the pace their lives were moving at meant that Tom would have to apply for his test immediately.

He was told, when he went for the application form at the post office, that it could take up to three weeks, before a test place was available. In the meantime, Jennifer knew that she would have to give Tom as much practice as her nerves could cope with. She was dreading having to take him through a built-up area, but that would have to be faced and that was all there was to it. Fortunately, Stanley her father's chauffeur, come general handyman, whom Tom liked, stepped in at her mother's suggestion, and took over Tom's lessons.

Chapter Sixteen

Jennifer's appointment, with Doctor Hart, was at 8:30am.

Neither of them had slept well, they had lain still, each trying not to disturb the other. Eventually Tom said, 'I can't sleep and I know you are awake too, can I make you a cup of tea.'

'Thanks Tom, I'll get up with you.' They went into the kitchen.

'You sit at the table, I'll make it.'

'I don't understand it Tom, I feel so good, and I have since we met up again.' Tom turned to her and set her mug of tea on the table.

'I don't suppose you have recovered.'

'I just don't know Tom; I don't even want to think that – it's too much to hope for. We will simply have to wait to hear what Mrs Hart has to say tomorrow.' Tom reached across the table and squeezed her hand.

'I'll be with you, come what may, that's the deal remember.'

'I know Tom, but it's too much to ask you to suffer like this, I should never have come to the gallery that day.'

'Jen, I really can't explain it, this is hell, but I can't live without you either. I don't understand any of it. All I can think is that this is the price, or cost of loving. I think of the hits we deal out to our parents and they just take them. They have no defence; love in some way makes us defenceless. I keep thinking about that preacher chap saying to us that God is constantly asking, "Do you know that I love you". In spite of the fact we crucified Him, I kind of understand that, because of what I feel for you. Whatever, all I can say is, do you know that I love you. No matter what happens, suppose you hated me and rejected me, I would still be saying, do you know that I love you.'

'Tom, you are so beautiful, how I thank God for you.'

'Come on, it's too early for all this deep stuff, let's see if we can catch some more shut-eye.'

They were at the hospital before the appointed time. The receptionist asked them to take a seat and they were told a nurse would be with them directly. Over the course of the morning, Jennifer was subjected to all manor of prodding and poking, including x-rays, with a liberal dose of blood letting.

Eventually they were taken to Mrs Hart's office, the nurse knocked on her door, and they were shown in. The Doctor stood and shook hands with Jennifer and Jennifer introduced Tom.

'Pleased to meet you Mr Jackson, do take a seat. You are looking well Jennifer, how do you feel?' The doctor asked.

'I feel wonderful Doctor,' the doctor smiled. Jennifer answered the questions, and the doctor made notes. Tom watched the doctor's hand; it seemed to write without her ever taking her eyes off Jennifer. Her appearance was one of total care and concern. When Jennifer had said all, the doctor set down her pen and paused for a moment running her finger lightly back and forth along the length of the pen as it lay on her notepad.

'Mmm, I'm please that you are so well at this time. This is what is commonly known as a remission.'

'What does that mean?' Tom blurted out.

'Tom, may I call you Tom?' Tom nodded, 'We don't know why this happens, perhaps an emotional change, releasing, for example, a surge of hormones into the system, who knows, there is no scientific medical explanation, but what you are experiencing is not uncommon. It is an apparent reversal of the disease process, sometimes brought about by treatment or spontaneously.'

'Could – I – be healed?' Jennifer asked hesitantly.

'Mmm, nothing is impossible, but it would be wrong of me to give improbable hope. Sadly, by the nature of the word, a *remission* is not a cure. I must tell you this, the disease is still present but not so intrusive. I'm sorry, but I want you to have confidence, that what I am telling you is always the truth, as I see it. I promise, that when you leave my office, you never need to be worried that I am keeping something from you. It is my firm conviction, that this is the kindest approach and you can then make what plans you want, with confidence.'

'Thank you Doctor, I am much happier with that, and I'm sure you are too, Jennifer,' Tom said turning to Jennifer and she nodded.

'My advice is to make the most of the moment, live your life. I will be able to tell you more, once I have some results back from the tests today. As it is nearing Christmas, I will do my utmost to write to your G.P. before the holiday so that you will not "Be left up in the air", so to speak, over the festive period. Is there anything else you would like to ask me? Don't be afraid to ask whatever is on your mind, no matter how trivial you think it to be.'

They looked at each other. 'I have a thousand questions, but my brain is at sixes and sevens at this moment. We are getting married two days before Christmas, is there anything you want to say about that?' asked Tom.

'Certainly, congratulations, have a wonderful time. Here,' she wrote a number on a scrap of paper, 'this number will reach me, if you think of anything once you have gone, call me. Believe me, I understand. Actually, my husband had this illness, so I do appreciate the stress you are under. I don't normally mention this, and I don't know why I have now, very unprofessional. Forgive me.'

They thanked the doctor and left, strangely, feeling better. What more could the poor lady have said, it was actually a comfort knowing she truly understood.

Chapter Seventeen

Jennifer walked up to Tom on her father's arm; it was hardly the aisle in the cathedral. Tom didn't care a fig, she was smiling as he turned, and she looked... breathtaking. She was the embodiment of every love poem he had ever read, rolled into one, and he loved her.

She came to his side, took his hand and reached up to his ear and whispered, 'I'm pregnant.'

'WHAT!' Tom's exclamation was heard all over the room, the Registrar leant forward and asked if everything was all right. 'Err, yes, yes, I do.'

'I haven't asked you anything, yet Thomas,' the Registrar responded.

'Oh, sorry, I do.'

'Thomas, I have to ask you first.' Jennifer almost laughed aloud.

'Do you wish for a moment to collect yourselves?'

'No, no, what's next?'

The poor fellow just sighed and began. 'We are gathered...' It was all over in moments, when it actually came to the place where Tom was expected to respond, he looked as if he was in another world, and Jennifer had to tug his hand before he collected himself and said "I do". Tom was so agitated he couldn't remember a thing, suddenly they were signing the register, cameras flashed, and he was walking out of the place with yellow flashes in his eyes. At the entrance before they stepped outside, there was a toilet, Tom pushed the door open and bundled his new wife in.

'This is all new to me, I have never been in a gentleman's toilet before,' Jennifer laughed.

'What! Oh, never mind that, what do you mean you are pregnant?'

'Just that, I'm pregnant, and, I am delighted.'

'But, you said you couldn't get pregnant.'

'Hmm, there you go, I am, for sure.'

There was a knock on the door and Tom's brother called, 'Ye aall reet in there?'

'Yes, yes, just give us a second,' Tom called back.

'It's just that the photographer's waiting, de ye want him to come in there?'

'Ha, ha, very humorous, we'll be with you in a minute.'

'Ye de naa ye are in the "Gent's"?'

'Yes, now will you go away Fred, and have your picture taken, we have things to discuss.' Jennifer couldn't contain her laughter; in fact, she struggled so much, her stifled laughter turned into hiccups.

'Ah, this is hopeless. What about your treatment Jen, how does this effect everything.' She placed her finger on his lips, and tried to control herself.

'Tom, I knows nothing, but I am happy, happy,' and she kissed him.

'You are a nutcase, Mrs Jackson, what does that make me? I'm in love with a nutcase. Come on let's face the maddening crowd.' When they did make it outside, they were met with puzzled faces. Tom thought that his apparent odd behaviour would confirm Jennifer's family's worst doubts, about the man she had chosen.

'Right,' said the photographer from the Gazette, who was a colleague of Jennifer's. 'We'll just take a couple here, as it's cold and starting to snow, then we will take more at the reception.'

Tom was still struggling to think of anything other than that Jennifer was pregnant, what would his in-laws think, what a nightmare. Yet, every time he looked at Jennifer she appeared as if she didn't have a care in the world, it was all quite mad, mad.

Tom had ordered top hat and tails for himself and his brothers. Jennifer said he must wear whatever he wanted, but he wanted it to be perfect for her, and he was determined to make as much effort for her, as she had for him. Besides, Tom hated the way wedding photographs dated and that very special memory became the subject of laughter because of the clothes. It was true; today's trend could look utterly ridiculous, even a mere ten years "Down the road". Morning suits were timeless and that's what he wanted this moment to be. He knew he would look at these photographs many times in the future and they would never date, always fresh. Nope, morning suits were the only option for him and he didn't care in the least what anyone thought. He knew some of his friends, and perhaps even his family would think he was "Getting above himself". It's hard cheese, he thought, that's just tough, he knew Jennifer would be pleased, and that was more than enough reason.

There were further surprises; Tom couldn't believe how articulate his brother was. Tom had been nervous about him speaking; he didn't want Fred to look foolish in front of Jennifer's family and friends. As it turned out Fred was brilliant, when it was his turn to speak, he made everyone laugh. He started his speech by saying, 'A hev only been a "Best man" once before, and that was for a fellow who was a member of the haemorrhoid society. The meal after was a stand up buffet".'

Once again, Tom wondered why he knew so little about his brother. All those years he'd missed, how could you live with someone, see him everyday, and know so little. Tom supposed that he was always too full of himself, and felt quite ashamed. It simply affirmed what he already knew, he'd learnt more about his brothers and sister, since he had introduced Jennifer to them, than ever he knew before. She seemed to be interested in people, and people responded, it always appeared effortless to her. He noticed when one was with Jennifer that person was the only person in the world, or that's what it seemed like.

Tom turned to Jennifer, 'I love you.'

'I know.'

'But you *can't* possibly know how much.'

'Yes I do,' and she leaned over from her seat and kissed him much to the enjoyment of the guests.

Jennifer, who had insisted that Tom's niece Peggy was a bridesmaid, whom incidentally, Tom thought stole the show, she was so enchanting.

Fred's speech was at the other end of the scale to his new father-in-law's rambling discourse. It was poor in the extreme, the unfortunate fellow looked to be totally out of his depth. Tom thought he sounded like he was delivering the annual report to the board of the shipyard, and the shares were down, it was that scintillating. Those awake at the end politely applaud.

Jennifer's friends and relations were actually very welcoming. The reception was at Jennifer's home. Because of the speed everything was happening, it was the only option.

Tom didn't know whether to smile or cringe, when her aunt, asked Jennifer where she found her husband, 'He looks like a film star, he could double for Sean Connery, you know 007, lucky you.'

They had a band in the evening and as they danced, it was obvious to Tom, Jennifer was amused at what her aunt had said, and she whispered in his ear, 'I think you are more handsome, in fact I can see you as Mr Bond, in your top hat and tails, all suave and sophisticated, not shaken but stirred.' Jennifer whispered in his ear.

Tom smiled and pulled his head back to look at her, 'Believe me, you will see me both shaking and stirred when we have to tell your mum and dad, the good news about their grandchild, it will be a greater challenge than ever Mr Bond had to face with "Dr. No". It will confirm all your dad's suspicions, and we will have been marked down as liars.'

'It will be fine, we'll wait a month before we tell them.'

'I think you'll still struggle to sell them that one. Changing the subject from my film career, I'm sorry not to give you a proper honeymoon. I will make it up to you, when we go to London, for the exhibition in January.'

'As far as the honeymoon goes, Tom, we are going to our own house tonight, then it's Christmas, honestly I could not be happier,

AND, we are having a baby, that is as good as it gets.'

'Jen, I can't believe that you dropped that one on me, as we stood before the Registrar. I was nervous enough as it was. Why didn't you just whack me with a hammer if you wanted to get a reaction?' Jennifer laughed.

'I had only found out, Doctor Hart rang me. She said it had shown up in the tests they carried out the other day. Sorry, sweetheart, I didn't intend to. I was so excited it merely slipped out, I could have bit my tongue, when I said it, but you know what?'

'What, don't tell me there is more?'

'No,' she smiled, 'I can't top that, but it was worth it to see your face. It brings a smile to my face every time I think of it. You will remember that moment for the rest of your life.'

'I think I will, it might make you smile but, it will forever bring me out in a cold sweat. You amaze me girl, you can always draw the positive out of everything, have I told my new wife I love her?'

'Don't think you have.'

'I wonder what make of baby we are having, I can't get my head around this.'

'I want a boy, Tom.'

'Not so loud, Jen, your mum never misses a thing. Me, I want a girl, the double of her mum.'

'Yes... it will be a girl; of course it will... it's obvious isn't it. Let's go Tom, I'm going to cry, I need you to hold me and love me, I feel safe in your arms. I can't say goodbye to everyone, I'll cry, reality has just walked in and kicked me in the gut. I don't want to dampen people's fun with my tears and make a fool of myself, let's just sneak away.'

'Look, you make your way out, I'll explain to your mum, she will make our excuses.'

Chapter Eighteen

'What else can one say Jen, as years go, this has been different, or perhaps this is normal for you?'

'Not really Tom, this year has been the darkest and the brightest I have ever known from the heights to the depths. I have to tell you Tom, it doesn't get any better than sitting here in front of this roaring log fire with your arms around me, knowing I am expecting our baby.'

They were both sitting on the floor. The only light in the room was from the fairy lights on the Christmas tree and the log fire. Tom was leaning against the settee and Jennifer was sat between his legs, lying against his chest. Tom's cheek rested against the side of Jennifer's head and his arms were wrapped around her.

'Once this is over it will be all go, we have the exhibition in London straight after Christmas. After which we will be home for a short break, it won't be a holiday because we will have to prepare for the trip to New York. Are you sure you are up to all this, Jen?'

'What can I say, I feel good at this moment, that's all I know and I will go with that? I will never sit in a basket chair. I am going to enjoy every moment of our life.'

They were to go to the big house for lunch on Christmas day and in the evening, Tom's sister had organised a party at her house.

'Come on, let's cut off a chunk of the Christmas cake your mum sent and have a glass of something. Living next to your mum is like living next to Fortnum and Mason's, she is always sending us treats.' Tom pulled Jennifer up and they went into their kitchen.

'Good old Mummy, she is kind and I have been horrid to her lately.'

'Oh,' Tom frowned, 'when?'

'Awe, let's forget that, it's just that it was difficult when we separated and poor mummy suffered for it, I'm afraid, but let's not dwell there.'

'Ah.'

Jen removed the cake from the box whilst Tom poured two glasses of sherry.

'We are not staying late at Molly's when we go, Jen, you need to rest, you know how tired you are.'

'I think that this is all pretty normal. I know you are right but I feel so happy. I want to tell everybody about our baby, it's going to be a challenge to keep it to myself all over Christmas, Christmas is about babies isn't it?'

'I know all about how difficult it is for you to keep that secret. I discovered that on our wedding day. Boy, is your timing ace, how I didn't collapse right in front of that Registrar, I will never know. Thank goodness I don't have a weak heart.'

'Awe, I am awfully sorry about that, Tom, *darling, sweetheart*. As I told you before, it just slipped out.'

'It just slipped out did it, *darling, sweetheart*? Oh, that's all right then,' and Jen laughed.

'I have told you before woman, apologies lose all credibility when you are laughing,' and he grabbed her by the waist and began to playfully bite at her neck.

'TOM, TOM, you're giving me goose pimples all over,' she said laughing, and wriggling to be free.

'Now, where is that rock pool, you're just lucky it's not near here. I haven't forgotten I owe you a ducking,' still holding her by the waist, he lifted her off the ground until their lips met and kissed her.

'I love you, Mr Jackson, I love you, I love you, I love you. Can I open my present now, it's almost Christmas day?'

'No.'

'Spoil sport.'

'It's three hours until Christmas day and we are going to bed with our drink and cake, total decadence, and I like it just fine. I will lay aside my socialist principles for this evening.'

'Wake up, wake up.'

'What, what is it?' Tom said lifting the bed covers off his head, 'What is it?'

'It's Christmas, it's Christmas, I can open my present now.'

'Is that it, I thought that the house was on fire, I was on a desert island with a beautiful woman.'

'Oh, and who was that may I ask?'

'Guess,' and he lifted himself up and kissed her.

'Come on, let's go downstairs, I left the heating on so it would be nice and warm.'

Tom's gift to Jennifer was in a large box and she excitedly tore at the wrapping. There was another box inside that. She looked puzzled. She tore into that one. Then there was another, then another, and another, until there was a very small box.

'Tom, what is it!'

'Mmm, I wonder.'

She opened it ever so nervously; when she lifted the lid, the Christmas tree lights instantly brought life to the diamonds.

'Oh Tom... it's gorgeous, an eternity ring,' she struggled to speak, and tears began to trickle down her face. 'How long will that be, Tom?'

'Just that, for eternity, I wouldn't have bought it if I had known you wouldn't like it.'

'I love it,' she whispered slipping it onto her finger.

'No tears then, you can't imagine the dangers I went through to get it. I had to go back to the jeweller's where we got your engagement ring, against my better judgement, I might add, but I knew they would know your ring size and you might have guessed it, our friendly assistant came straight to me.'

Jennifer's face was now transformed into laughter, 'He probably thought you were coming for a date.'

'Ha, ha, not funny, so I bought the first one he showed me.'

'It's magnificent, thank you. I love it.' Jennifer passed Tom her present for him; it was a bigger box than the one that contained Jennifer's ring, perhaps four inches square.

'Hmm, it's not a ring, unless it's a whopper.'

'Come on, open it.' Tom removed the paper and flipped open the box lid. It was a gold watch. He carefully removed it.

'Wow, a gold Rolex Oyster, wow,' he repeated himself, 'Tom from Waterloo Terrace, a committed socialist with a "Gold Rolex", what will the party leader think?' he joked.

'From what I know of socialists, he's probably already got one,' Jennifer said and Tom laughed. He took it out of the box, removed the one he was wearing, slid the Rolex bracelet onto his wrist and closed the clasp.

'Thanks Darling, I love it. Need I say I have never had anything like this? I shudder to think how much this has cost.' He stroked around the bezel lovingly with his thumb, 'What on earth will your mum and dad think? I had better not let them see it.'

'It was mummy's idea; I couldn't think what to buy you. I wanted to buy you something *very* individual to remember me by, something you would have all your life and look at several times a day, every day, is that terribly selfish, Tom?'

'Don't say that, not today.'

'Sorry Tom,' he took her in his arms and they held each other.

Tom coughed and cleared his throat, 'Come on, there are more presents, let's make a pot of tea and come back and finish the work of opening them.' They came back and sat again on the floor, there was the usual mix of chocolates, slippers, gloves, shirts, make-up, presents that all the family had given. They tidied up the wrapping paper and washed up the cups they had left in the kitchen the night before, dressed and went up to the big house for lunch. Tom was quite surprised, the place was full of people, most, Tom vaguely recognised from their wedding but hadn't a clue what they were called. Actually, they made him feel very welcome, they came and chatted to him as if he was just one of the family, which he supposed he was.

'Hello James,' Jennifer's Aunt Susan said to him smiling and kissed him.

'Leave him alone, Aunt, he's mine.' Jennifer laughed. Tom was genuinely surprised how friendly they all were, even Lord Peter had managed some civil festive conversation. He was glad that Jennifer hadn't forewarned him what it would be like or he would have worried himself sick. They all admired Jennifer's ring. Tom was constantly nervous that Jennifer would not be able to prevent her joy overflowing and tell her family about their baby but she managed to resist the temptation.

When they left to travel to Molly's house for the next party, Tom said that she had done well not to let the cat out of the bag about their impending family.

'You will never know how hard that was, Tom,' Jennifer smiled at him. 'I'm frightfully relieved that we have had to go, I really don't know how much longer I could have held out.'

'You'll have it all to go through again now, at our Molly's.'

'I'm sure it would be all right to tell Molly.'

'Are you joking? You may as well put an article in your dad's paper, or even better, why not go national.' Jennifer laughed. 'No way, you keep shtum.'

The door opened as they walked up the path to Molly's front door.

'Howay, in, it's caad, oot there, a saw ya comin when a looked oot the window,' welcomed Jim, Molly's husband, hugging Jennifer. 'Here let me have ya coats.' They were directed into the front room. Peggy came straight to Jennifer wanting to be picked up. Tom quickly redirected her, picking her up and lifting her up to the ceiling.

'No kisses for your Uncle Tom then,' he asked tickling her. He didn't want Jennifer lifting her off the ground. 'Sit down Aunty Jen, apparently it's you who are the flavour of the month,' smiled Tom.

Every time Jennifer had seen Peggy, she had brought her a little present in her bag, and this was no exception. They had sent her main present through the week so it would be there for Christmas morning. Peggy sat on Jennifer's knee and Jennifer took out a little parcel from her handbag, all neatly wrapped. Tom smiled, Jen may be lacking in the cooking department, day-to-day cooking anyway, but when it came to wrapping up presents she was unequalled. Peggy glowed.

'Your Aunty Jennifer does spoil you,' Molly said, stroking Peggy's hair, 'What have you got now?' Peggy unwrapped the gift to reveal a little Steiff teddy bear; Peggy immediately hugged and kissed it.

'What do you say to Aunty Jennifer, Peggy?' Peggy threw her arms around Jennifer's neck and kissed her.

Fred noticed Tom's watch; Tom nervously tugged down his sleeve.

'Diven't ever be ashamed, bonny lad, of where you are, you have a grand lass there and we are all happy for you, she's one of us, family and we will always be here for you.'

'Thanks Fred, that means a lot.'

The rest of the evening was taken up with singing favourite Geordie songs, such as Cushie Butterfield and The Blaydon Races, whilst Fred played his accordion. Michael recited a monologue, which was a Geordie version of the Battle of Waterloo. It had always been a family favourite, the family's home having been in Waterloo Terrace.

Tom and Jennifer waved goodbye, having stayed far longer than he intended. Every time he had mentioned going, Jennifer had said, "Just a little longer". They didn't know when they would see them again for some time; it was London next and then New York.

'I have really enjoyed myself Tom; I have never known a time like that. Knowing you makes my life perfect, God is good, don't ever forget that will you, Tom?'

Chapter Nineteen

The first thing that needed to be attended to after Christmas was Tom's driving test, which he sailed through, or at least that was how he described the event. Jennifer congratulated him, but he couldn't resist asking her if she had passed her first test, knowing full well that she had failed.

'I'm not answering that, as you already know the answer and I have told you, it was a simple case of an examiner who didn't like women.'

'Oh, I'm sure it was.'

Jennifer narrowed her eyes and glared at him. 'Oh, you are such a bighead, Tom Jackson.'

'What do you mean, I'm agreeing with you, am I not?'

'That's the sort of agreeing that could get you a black eye, if you don't watch it.'

The contract with the Weltzman Institute had all been signed and dealt with before Christmas, by Tom's solicitor, Mr Henderson; very efficiently, Tom had to concede.

'I have to say Jennifer, money certainly greases the wheels of life, I could get used to this way of living. I would have been struggling and worrying about that contract, I mean ten thousand pounds is the sort of money people from Waterloo Terrace dream about; it's football pools payout type money. I have heard of people retiring, after winning the amount of money I have made from one exhibition.'

'And this is only the beginning. So what's it feel like to be a wealthy man, Tom?'

'Aye... as we know money can't buy everything. At one time, like most people, I would have said money like this, would have sorted out all my problems. How many times have I heard that said? I would trade it, everything, my talent, all of it, Jen, every penny...'

'Tom, we are not going down that road, we are far too busy enjoying life, right.'

'Yep, right, we would, if you would ever finish packing that case.'

'Is that all *you* are taking, that *one* holdall?'

'Yes.'

'Let me see, what's in there, Tom.'

'Look Jen, the taxi comes in half and hour, we haven't time for you messing about.'

'Open it.'

'Ah, flipping heck.' Jennifer had wanted to pack for them both, but Tom said he was not going to have her running about after him like his mother had run about after his father, plus he said, 'You are pregnant.' Once he had said it, he then looked around to see who had heard. They still had not told Jennifer's mother and father. Tom was sure Jennifer's mother knew. He was conscious of every glance she gave Jennifer, imagining she had some super powers, which he knew from personal experience mothers had.

Tom reluctantly opened his bag, and Jennifer emptied it onto the bed.
'Careful, I have just folded all those things,' Jennifer stared at the pathetic little bundle, then at him.
'Tom, this is ridiculous, get that other case off the top of the wardrobe and I will pack your things as I wanted to do in the first place.' Tom was about to stand his ground but Jennifer gave him an iced look, which radiated waves of the word "Non-negotiable".
'Okay, okay, and he rather petulantly dragged the case off the wardrobe and plonked it down on the bed, then flopped into the armchair by the window. Since the first time he had met Jennifer, no, he thought, second time, he felt annoyed with her. He had been looking after himself for years, or that's what it seemed like. He had done what he liked, when he liked, and he knew how to pack for a couple of weeks in London. All he

needed was a fresh pair of socks, some underpants, a couple of shirts, and his wash bag. He couldn't imagine what Jennifer was putting into her case. That was one of the reason teaching had been so irksome to him, his life had to run on lines, and that did not suit his personality at all. He sat quietly, Jennifer sensed the tension and she stopped packing his case, turned to him, and smiled; Tom refused to make eye contact.

'Tom Jackson! Do I detect a little sulk?'

'What! I have no idea what you are talking about.' She went over to him and sat on his knee, putting her arms around his neck. He was refusing to respond and she started to nibble at his ear, he resisted at first, but gradually he was fighting off a smile, then he laughed and picked her up cradling her in his arms, carried her to the bed and sat her down in the case.

'Look woman, as long as I have you in my case I have all I need.'

'So that's all I am to you, a pair of underpants.'

"BEEP, BEEP" a car horn sounded from outside.

'What did I tell you, it's the taxi,' with that he left Jennifer in the case and went to the window. 'Here's your mother too; she will have come to say goodbye, just as well because we wouldn't have had time to go up to the house.'

'Quick, help me out of here, it will slip off the bed and I'll fall on the floor and break something, my neck most probably. Then go down to the taxi, tell him we will be there in a moment and take my case with you. I'll finish packing this one.' Tom picked up Jennifer's case, gasping and groaning at the weight for effect. 'Err, Tom, what about me?'

'Opps.' Tom set the case down, and went to lift Jennifer out of his case. Once she was back on her feet, he took her case down to the taxi.

'Morning Carolyn.'

'Good morning, Tom.'

'Jen's messing about upstairs, still packing her case.'

'Good to see *you* are more organised, Tom.'

Tom smiled, 'I tried to tell her, but she wouldn't listen.'

'TOM JACKSON! I don't believe you said that,' Jennifer shouted down the stairs.

'Err, *must* crack on Carolyn.' He told the taxi driver they would be ready in a moment and went back inside for the other case. He slid his head around the bedroom door and smiled.

'Everything just about ready, *sweetheart*?'

'Thank you *sweetheart*, MY case is ready now,' she said narrowing her eyes at him. Tom smiled and shrugged his shoulders at Lady Carolyn, who laughed.

Tom carried the second case down and gave it to the taxi driver.

Lady Carolyn came downstairs to the front door and hugged them both before they climbed into the taxi, wishing them well with the exhibition.

Tom held the door of the taxi for Jennifer and before they knew it, they were on the train heading south.

'Are you excited?' Tom asked Jennifer.

'Yes, we certainly have an exciting life Tom. I keep trying to imagine my life, if you had not forgotten your haversack, all the happiness and laughter we have had, would not have been.' She came and sat by him and he put his arm around her. Jennifer had been sitting opposite him in the other window seat.

'You're missing the view now.'

'I don't care.'

'How are you feeling Jen, I haven't had time to ask this morning, what with all my packing?' she smiled and poked him.

'Actually, this continuous nauseous feeling in the mornings is not so pleasant, but apart from that, I don't feel any different.'

'No regrets?'

'No regrets, I'm happy.'

It was teatime when the train pulled into King's Cross Station. They had both slept on the journey down to London, which meant that the time seemed to pass quickly.

Mr Armstrong-Bennett had organised accommodation for them near to the gallery in the Strand. The taxi took them right to the door and the driver handed their cases to the concierge with his smart maroon uniform,

"Top hat" and white gloves. All very impressive Tom thought. Tom paid the taxi driver, and then grumbled.

'Fllllllliping heck, that cost an arm and a leg, Jen. I think I have just bought shares in that taxi firm.'

'Oh, I thought it seemed reasonable.'

'Maybe in your circles, but not for a lad from Waterloo Terrace, it was daylight robbery.'

'Tom, you are such an inverted snob.'

'No, I'm just proud of me roots, bonny lass.'

'It appears that these are *your* circles now,' Jennifer said looking up at the hotel façade, 'I'm merely the *wife* of a famous artist.'

'Give over, I feel more like a conman, who's struck it lucky, I'll wake up in a minute and be back at school, standing before 3b and terrified of them, heaven's above, what a thought.' They went to the desk and asked about their room.'

'Mmm,' the man at the desk said, as he scanned down the list of guests, 'ah, yes, Mr Jackson and Mrs Jackson, is that correct?'

'Err, yes that's right.'

'Room 214, it's on the second floor, the lift is over there,' he pointed, 'I will see to your luggage. There is a sheet there with information about meals etcetera. If you require any further help, there is a telephone in your room; merely ring reception and someone will attend to you directly. Oh, yes, I nearly forgot, one more thing, Sir, there is a letter here for you.' He turned to some pigeonholes behind him to retrieve a letter and passed it to Tom. Tom looked at it, back, and front, but it only had his name on it. He thanked the man at the desk and they made their way up to their room. He opened the door, 'Wow, this is all right, Jen,' he said looking around the room.

'Yes, it's very nice I must agree Tom, Reginald has chosen well.'

Tom bounced on the bed, 'Wow, this is a bit posh, and we have even got a toilet and bath in the bedroom, I'm not sure about that. Do you know Jen, this is the first proper hotel I have ever stayed in.'

'They are not actually *in* the bedroom Tom, to be perfectly accurate. Anyway, didn't you have a bath in the front room, at your idyllic hideaway by the sea? Home from home,' Jennifer laughed as she lay down beside him.

'Ha, you jest, but I must say, I will love that place until the day I die. Now let me take a look at this letter, probably the bill.' Tom tore it open, 'Ah, it's from Reginald, he writes that he looks forward to seeing us at the gallery tomorrow and hopes that our accommodation is satisfactory. I think we can make do with it, Lady Jennifer.'

'I'm going to bathe, in that enormous bath, will you join me Mr Jackson?'

'Do you know, I think I might, shall *we* phone down to the jolly old chap on the desk, for some jolly old back scrubbers? Perhaps *not* this time.'

The next morning Mr Armstrong-Bennett was already at the gallery when Tom and Jennifer walked in. He smiled and came to greet them.

'Good morning, delighted to see you again,' he said offering his hand. 'What do you think, is it to your liking,' he gestured with his hand to the exhibition. They both looked around.

'Very impressive, Reginald, it's strange how the presentation of work can add such credibility to it, suddenly a piece of canvas with some daubs of paint on it becomes "Art", it's all about the illusion.'

'Ha, I have told you before, you don't realise how talented you are, this work is truly exceptional, we only try to show it in a way that the viewer sees it at it's best. Yes, I must say I'm very satisfied. We open at ten, and then we will see how successful our advertising has been. In the mean time can I offer you some refreshment?'

'Certainly.' Mr Armstrong-Bennett led them to the cafeteria. Over coffee he told Tom there would be people from the press coming sometime this morning for a interview, 'So you may wish to think about that Tom, and you too, Lady Jennifer, no doubt they will be interested in your comments. Once we have finished you can wander as you see fit, I will be back and forth if you have any questions. In the mean time, I will leave you in the capable hands of Irene, she is responsible for the exhibition, and the one to see if you have any queries, but she has not arrived yet.' After the coffee, they all went back to the room where Tom's work was displayed, and walked around. They saw a lady enter with a package under her arm, Reginald smiled at her and told them this was Irene and introduced them.

'I'm sorry I'm late but I had to call at the printers for these posters, they promised to deliver them, but such is life.'

Tom and Jennifer continued looking at the paintings, leaving Irene to do whatever she had to do.

'I can't get my mind around this Jen, it is the weirdest thing seeing my work framed, it's quite surreal in a way.'

'They do look astonishing, Tom. I love them, isn't it thrilling? I like that grand piano over there,' Jennifer said nodding, 'it's a Steinway, I have never actually played one. I wonder Reginald, would anyone mind terribly if I made the most of this opportunity and played it?'

'Certainly my dear lady, you are more than welcome, you honour us.'

'What! You play the piano, another secret, boy, oh boy,' Tom said looking incredulously at Jennifer.

'Yes, I play a little.' The gallery was beginning to fill with visitors. Jennifer sat at the piano and began to play. Tom was "Gob smacked", she was absolutely brilliant;

people all turned to her and simply stood and listened.

'Everything about you two is original. This has never happened before,' Reginald said, '*and,* we have an illustrious visitor I see, a friend of yours, is he?'

'Sorry, what do you mean?'

'That young man there,' Reginald nodded his head discreetly in the direction of a young man with longish sandy coloured hair and heavy black-rimmed spectacles.

'No, I'm sorry, I don't know the man.'

'I think you probably do, it's none other than John Lennon of The Beatles.'

'No... really... do you know, I think you are right, Reginald. I wonder if Jen knows who is listening to her playing.'

'He may not recognise the piece, but *I* adore it, it's a piece by Frédéric Chopin, clearly John Lennon likes beautiful music.'

'I don't know much about classical music I'm afraid. Do you know what it is?' Tom whispered.

'Yes, it's Nocturne Opus 9, number 1 in B flat minor, Magnificent, quite magnificent.'

'Mmm, I think the Beatles have a better line in titles.'

Gradually, the music enhanced by the acoustics of the hall, engulfed Tom, he was totally mesmerised, everything faded from his consciousness and he was alone with Jennifer, and this heavenly sound, in some dream place.

When Jennifer finished, there was complete silence, as if those who listened were fearful of breaking the magic spell she had cast. One by one, those gathered began to clap and the applause grew louder and louder, with calls asking for more. Jennifer stood, bowed, and smiled; thanking them, saying that she hoped they enjoyed her husband's exhibition.

Tom was overcome, he could hardly speak; for him this had been one of the most moving moments in the whole of his life, listening to her play. He went to her and hugged her, then stepped back with his hands on her shoulders, holding her at arms length, only able to shake his head, his eyes were full of tears.

'I love you, what on earth were you thinking of, marrying me. I will have to go to the cloakroom to wash my face in some cold water and try to drag myself back into this world. That was inspired. I can't tell you how the moment touched me.'

'I had to marry you or who would have packed your case,' Jennifer said smiling up at him.

All he could do was look at her; he leant forward and tenderly kissed her.

'And... I just happen to love you.' Tom jerked his head in acknowledgement and left her. After a few moments, Tom returned to see Jennifer talking to John Lennon, and he joined them.

'Ah, Tom, may I introduce you to Mr Lennon.'

'Pleased to meet you, people will think we have made it, shaking hands with a famous Beatle,' John Lennon smiled.

'Ha, famous, I'm just a fool on a hill. I was admiring your work, and was captured by the music, makes me feel like a busker. I think your work will be around long after the Beatles are forgotten.'

'I didn't recognise you in the glasses.'

'That's the plan; really I'm as blind as a bat without them, it seems to be all about image. If I fall over an amplifier the only thing that matters is, will it cost the promoters any cash. Anyway, I saw a poster in our hotel, advertising your exhibition and escaped for an hour. I try to get around all the galleries. I studied art at college, along with my friend Stuart.'

'He's not one of the Beatles, is he?' Tom asked.

'Awe... he was sort of, in the early days, but tragically he died.'

'Sorry to hear that,' Jennifer said.

'Yeah, it was a waste, I loved him, you don't know what pain is till you lose someone you really love; I've had my share of that joke. Anyway, that's me; hope you never find out about the crippling fun of losing someone before you're ready to say goodbye. The reason I'm talking to your wife, apart from thanking her for playing, is that I would like to purchase one of your pictures; it made me think of Stuart and my mum. I couldn't take my eyes off it, then I saw it was called,

"Without You", no wonder it got to me, that's the one over there.'

'Sure, it will be a pleasure to know that the picture belongs to someone who understood, you're very kind. I'm glad you liked it. I hate to think of my work, as no more than wallpaper, which matches the carpet or paintwork.

Let me introduce you to Irene, she is handling sales, no doubt she will be delighted to help you.'

'Thanks, I think your work is really fab, best of luck.' Tom took him over to Irene, who seemed to lose her faculties, and Tom returned to Jennifer, smiling.

'Fancy, he could feel that picture, and understood,' Tom said looking quite at a loss.

'What a nice sensitive, gentle, man, I really liked him. Not the mindless young pop idol, the media try to portray,' Jennifer said.

'I'm not sure this world is a place for sensitive people, I hope it doesn't destroy him.'

Chapter Twenty

When Jennifer and Tom arrived home from London, they knew the first thing to be faced was granddad and grandma to be. Tom lifted their cases out of the taxi, paid the driver and they went into the Lodge.

'Do you want a cuppa, Jen?' Tom tried to make his offer sound casual.

'Look Tom, a cup of tea would be welcome, but how long can we keep putting this off. I am not going to be able to settle until we have told mummy and daddy that I am pregnant. I don't want mummy to become suspicious, and she will. Please can we go now, and tell them? We ought to go up to the house and let them know we are home, it would be inconsiderate not to. Mummy would expect us to let them know, she will have been worrying I know she will. It's not as if it's the middle of the night, we have no excuse for skulking in the house and hiding away. Anyway, we have no milk.'

'Ah, good point. Sorry Jen, you know me too well. It's just that they are going to blame me.'

'What do you mean, blame you?'

'They are going to think this is irresponsible, and they would be right, it is irresponsible, it will make your future treatment, if you need any, more complex.'

'Tom, this is our baby you are talking about, a life living in me, defencelessly dependent on me.' He came to put his arms around her. '*Don't* touch me.' Tom jerked back. 'I want this baby and it's my life, this baby, is my life and all that there will be of me, surely what I want counts for something. It's my gift to you all, all I have to give.'

'I'm sorry Jen... there are so many emotions wrapped up in this whole business.' Tom turned resting on the kitchen sink and looked out into the garden. 'It's difficult to forge any sort of track through the turmoil.'

'I want your support, suppose no one else understands, I need you too. Do you love me that much, enough to let me go?'

'Hmm,' Tom hung his head and turned back to face her. 'My love for you Jen, paralyses me I'm afraid. I really don't know how I will manage. I just can't imagine life without you. As I say this, I'm ashamed because I know what I have just said is all about me, me, me.'

'Tom, you plus me equals "Us" and us/we have been given this gift, I am happy and thrilled, I can't tell you how thrilled. I will go through anything for our baby. This is something I can actually fight for, and win. It's a glimmer of hope, can't you see?'

'What a woman you are, how many times do I have to say this, what on earth did I do to deserve you, I love you so very much.'

'I was thirsty and you gave me a drink, I was hungry and you gave me a fish, remember.'

'Aye, I remember, that night and always will.'

'Actually, I was quoting a Christian tract, more or less, that had been left by my seat on the train when we travelled home.'

'Ah, it's still true, can I hug you now?'

'Let *me* hug *you*, then can we go to the big house.'

They strolled nervously hand in hand the short distance up to Jennifer's mother and father's house. Warwick greeted them, and informed them that Lady Carolyn was in the conservatory tying up some plants and they made their way through.

'Oh Jennifer, Tom, you're home.' Lady Carolyn smiled, removed her gardening gloves, and hugged them both. 'Come through into the warmth, I'm just tidying up in here everything gets such a mess in the winter. I'll organise some tea and you can tell of your adventure. Your father's in his study, let him know you're home, would you be so kind, and tell him there is tea on its way to the sitting room.' Jennifer called her father; he set his work aside giving them a token welcome and came to join them for tea.

'Nothing like a log fire this time of year, Jimmy and Phil took down the old beech tree in the paddock, it should keep us going in logs for this winter,' said Jennifer's father warming his hands. He turned to face them and continued to stand in front of the fire.

'Ah, here's mummy with the tea.'

'Just put it down there, Beth,' Lady Carolyn said pointing to an occasional table, ' I will attend to it.'

'Is that everything, my Lady?'

'Yes, thank you, that's perfect.' The girl bobbed and left.

'So, sit down and tell all,' Lady Carolyn said as she poured out the tea and passed them each a cup.

Jennifer proceeded to tell them how successful the exhibition had been. Tom made a great deal about Jennifer's contribution and how she was joining the Beatles, by request of John Lennon. Both Jennifer's mother and father had heard of the Beatles, but Tom could see blank faces at the mention of John Lennon's name, clearly, it didn't impress them. Jennifer was at pains to explain to them that Tom was making a joke.

'Ahhh,' said her father. 'So the exhibition was financially successful,' he carried on.

'Most successful, from every aspect, not only monetarily, Sir, but that aside, we have priceless news, which all the money in the world couldn't buy. We are having a baby.'

"Silence..."

'When is it due?' Jennifer's father asked, *clearly* suspicious, feeling his previous assumption was about to be confirmed.

'*September,*' Jennifer replied as casually as she could, she had been prepared for this.'

'Mmm,' was all he said.

'How wonderful darling,' Jennifer's mother said, once the initial shock had passed over. 'Congratulations,' and she got up and hugged them again.

'What about you, Daddy?'

'Naturally, of course, congratulations, when did you find out?'

'Err, a day or two ago, I spoke to Doctor Hart from London.'

'How did she know?'

'Is all this really important,' Tom jumped in, desperate to move things on and rescue Jennifer, who was floundering. What a tangled web we weave, when at first, we practice to deceive, or words to that effect, went through his head. 'We are thrilled and yes, I/we understand what is ahead, but we were always determined we would live our lives fully and this is part of our love.'

Jennifer reached up and kissed Tom and Lady Carolyn dabbed her eyes with her handkerchief.

'Your father smelt a rat, Jen,' Tom said as they walked back to their house. 'However, it matters not, he will just have to put it in his pipe and smoke it, like it or lump it as my mother used to say.'

'Thank you for all your love, Tom, I'm awfully sorry I was cross with you earlier, but this means so much to me and I really do feel well.'

'It was kind of your Mum to ask us to dinner, as you reminded me, we have nothing in, and I don't feel like going out. She's okay I like her. I'm going to be a *dad*, and the cat's out of the bag, now that feels pretty neat. Or as you would say, *awfully, frightfully*, neat.'

'Na, whey, it's grand, I'm a Geordie tee ye naas,' they both laughed.

Chapter Twenty-One

The plane tickets arrived by post. Now they had all the documentation and flight details, the plan would be to make their way to London by train, stay overnight then travel on to Gatwick and fly to Kennedy Airport in New York.

This would be Tom's first time in an aeroplane and he was filled with a mixture of fear and excitement. His feelings were overshadowed by his concern for Jennifer. Though she seemed well, she *was* pregnant and in the normal course of events, pregnancy involved a considerable degree of risk, but in Jennifer's case, the risk was serious, to both her, and their baby. Tom's thoughts were consumed by "What ifs". He had expressed his fears to Jennifer but, she would not relent, she was determined to go with him and that apparently was that. She said he needed to go to be seen with his work, to give interviews to the press, and talk to whoever was there. He *had* to go and she was not going to be separated from him. Of course, he couldn't contemplate the thought of being separated either, but he was sure this was foolish. Doctor Hart had told them to do whatever Jennifer felt able to do. It seemed that life had cornered him and the decision was taken out of his hands.

It would be Jennifer's birthday, three days after their scheduled return from New York. Tom decided he'd distract himself from his immediate fears, by buying Jennifer a very special gift. After much deliberation, he made the decision to purchase a Steinway piano, a baby *grand* piano.

He slipped away for the afternoon, on the pretext of seeing the dentist and went to the main music shop in Newcastle. He picked the piano he wanted, it was even more expensive than he had imagined. It would have to be ordered, but the salesman assured Tom that it would be delivered to his address on time.

He paid the man by cheque and organised for the delivery to be coordinated with Lady Carolyn. He didn't care how much it cost; he had the money and what would he need all this money for, if Jennifer died? He would do all in his power to make whatever time she had left, the most enjoyable and happy he possibly could, even if it cost every penny he earned.

Tom was smiling as he walked out of the shop, feeling pleased with himself, imagining Jennifer's face on the morning of her birthday, when *suddenly* he was enveloped by the dark ever-present cloud. The happiness he felt was suddenly dashed with thoughts of her not being here, and all the joy of the moment evaporated into a tormented vision of a life without her. Not for a week, not for a year, forever, he was overwhelmed.

The smile left his face, he was now merely being jostled and bumped along by the bustling shoppers. All his senses seemed to close down, he couldn't hear, feel or smell, even the information coming through his eyes, was not sparking any life into his brain.

This had happened several times now; it appeared that he was quite powerless to prevent it. He was learning to recognise the triggers, which brought about this debility, with the aim of avoiding them, but he was forever caught out, just a breath of her perfume was enough. *This,* was such a moment, he had relaxed his guard and allowed himself, just for a split second, to think about the years ahead. He would *never, ever* see, hear or touch her again, *never*, how could he live on without her. That was all it took, just a second and the weight of his fears overwhelmed him.

He was abruptly brought back into the now, when he stepped obliviously from the pavement onto the busy road. There was a screeching of brakes, and a car horn sounded, somewhere far off in his head, he could hear shouting. A man had rolled down his car window and was shouting abuse at him. Tom only stared at the man. At first, he was unable to move then his brain, working on "Auto pilot", took over and he slowly stepped back onto the pavement. He was lost, he looked around trying to recognise where he was. He leant against a wall and waited until he felt able to move on.

He caught the bus home, and was thankful to sit down and have this time to clear his head before he had to see Jennifer.

When he arrived home, Jennifer naturally asked if his trip to the dentist had been satisfactory, 'You still look a little dazed, probably the anaesthetic,' she said, stroking his cheek affectionately.

Without thought, merely reacting out of desperation, he grasped her roughly in his arms and held her tightly, 'Jen I love you. I'm not coping with this at all. I can't bear it, the thought of you not been here, cripples me.'

'Tom, please, we can't think like this it, will steal our time together. Remember the swallows, one moment at a time. This is the moment now, you are holding me and it's wonderful, I'm soaring, it's breathtaking I actually know what it is to be in love, kiss me.' He kissed her passionately as if it was their last kiss; he kissed her face, her eyes her hair.

'I love you Jen, I can't believe that everyone experiences this, the world would be a different place if people knew this love.'

'I love you, I love you,' Jennifer laughed and took his face in her hands. 'My dearest beautiful husband, how I love you. You are probably a touch low because of your trip to the dentist, it's never pleasant.'

Tom felt guilty at having to fabricate a story, but his conscience was satisfied that, in this case the end justified the means. He knew he would have to involve Lady Carolyn in the deception and hoped she would acquiesce.

Once again, they were packing; this time he left Jennifer in charge, once bitten twice shy, he had learnt from their last trip. She had proven to be better at that task than he was. His wardrobe had grown, he now had to think what to wear, it had never been an issue in his past life, he had only ever needed one change, now he found he had different functions to attend and each seemed to require different clothes. Jennifer was proving to be invaluable, he had never bothered about his clothes, he was never that interested, even though he was an artist his talents seemed to stop short of dress sense.

His time had been taken up liasing with Mr Armstrong-Bennett; together they decided what artwork was going to be shipped out to the gallery in New York. There was the packing too, which also needed to be overseen. They were extremely busy; Tom had agreed a time-frame for the exhibition, which was tight. Mr Armstrong-Bennett had been very obliging and sympathetic, once

Tom had explained all the complications. As far as Jennifer was concerned, it merely demonstrated how passionate he was about Tom's work. She was convinced Mr Armstrong-Bennett would not, perhaps have been so understanding, if Tom's work had been simply "Run of the mill". She knew that Tom still couldn't see that his work was anything extraordinary.

Having travelled by train to London, they made their way to a hotel near the airport, which had established itself for the precise purpose of accommodating air travellers. The hotel had even organised a shuttle bus to the airport as part of their package. Tom and Jennifer could have spent time in the city, but having only recently been to London they agreed that they would simply rest before the long journey to New York.

Everything ran like clockwork and before they knew it, they were clinging onto their seats speeding down the main runway at Gatwick.

The speed of the plane just prior to taking off was a complete new experience to both, Tom and Jennifer. Neither of them had ever experienced such forces pressing them back into their seats, they were both thrilled and exhilarated.

Once airborne Tom smiled at Jennifer and said, 'Wow, that was something else Jen, I have never felt anything quite like that, what about you? Are you alright?'

'Much the same as you, I supposed Tom, I'm still trying to get my breath back.'

'I fancy this trip will be a whole world of new experiences, come to think of it, that's my life's story since I met you.'

'This is all new to me too Tom, but I wouldn't miss it for the world.'

Neither of them knew anything about air turbulence, fortunately the flight did not experience any. As far as Tom and Jennifer were concerned this was what flying amounted to. It was a good flight, the food was excellent, and they slept a little. The plane circled Kennedy Airport before it made its landing approach. Jennifer looked out of the window and excitedly pointed to the things she saw. She had to tell Tom that he was crushing her as he leant over to see what she was pointing at.

'Sorry about that Jennifer, but it's difficult for me to see out of that small window.'

This cityscape was unlike any they had seen before. A voice came over the speaker system instructing them to fasten their seatbelts, as the plane was about to land. They clasped each other's hand tightly in anticipation of this next experience. They watched the descent through the window, lower and lower, the ground grew ever nearer, and suddenly they were down. The plane juddered as it landed, it seemed to Jennifer and Tom as if it bounced several times before it settled. There was a shudder as the brakes took hold, the whole plane vibrated and it began to quickly reduce speed. They both breathed out, neither were conscious that they had been holding their breath. Gradually the plane ceased shaking and taxied to a standstill.

'Phewww, that was not for the faint hearted, Jennifer.'

'I'm sure my heart will slow down eventually, Tom, look my hands are trembling.'

They unbuckled their safety belts, shuffled out of their seat into the aisle, collected their hand luggage, and walked down the steps from the plane to a waiting bus, which took them to the main terminal. Once through customs, they asked directions to where they might get a taxi. They were directed to a yellow taxi, which it appeared that New Yorkers called cabs. The cab took them to their hotel on Lexington Avenue. The art gallery was on Madison Avenue nearby, just off Central Park.

A man, on the door of the hotel, came quickly to the taxi to assist them with their luggage showing them to the reception desk.

Once they had signed the necessary documentation and shown their passports, they were given the keys to their room and directed to the "Elevator". They pressed number 14, the floor on which their room was located, the elevator doors closed, and up they went.

Once in their room, before they did anything else, they went to look at the view.

'I have never been in a building so high before, have you Jen?'

'No, I suppose it's safe.'

'Hmm, there seems to be a number of them around if they are not, and some are an awful lot higher than this one.'

'I feel along way from home and our little house, Tom.'

'We *are* a long way from home, it's hard to get your head around the miles we have travelled.'

'Where's the map the fellow downstairs gave you, he said it was easy to find your way around, the whole place is set out on a sort of grid.'

'I have the map here.' Tom set the map on the bed, they lay down, and looked at it, they found the gallery, which thankfully was not far away and next to that was Central Park.

'I think we should try to catch some sleep, Tom, I'm tired and my feet are swollen.'

'What, let me see.'

'Don't fuss Tom, I think it's pretty normal.' Jennifer undressed and climbed into the bed. Tom was in the bathroom washing, when there was a knock at the door.

'It's alright, I'll get it you lie still.' Tom opened the door; there was a bellboy there, who handed him a telegram. Tom mindlessly gave him a tip as he narrowed his eyes trying to make sense of the telegram.

'What is it Tom?' Tom didn't answer, Jennifer repeated her question, 'What is it Tom?'

'Oh, sorry Jen... it's a telegram, from your mother.' Jennifer was suddenly anxious and sat up.'

'A telegram, is something wrong?'

'She writes that a cheque I made out has "Bounced"; there was insufficient funds in the account to cover it. There must be some mistake.'

'What cheque?'

'Nothing important, I will have to try and give the bank a ring, *strange*, I can't understand it.'

This must be the cheque, I paid for Jen's piano, he thought, but I know there was plenty of money in the account to cover that. I specifically asked at the bank the day before.

'Tell you what Jen, you get some sleep, and I will go downstairs and see if I can ring the bank.'

'But Tom, the bank will be closed, it's 5:30am in England,' Jen said looking at her watch.'

'Oh blast, so it is. All the same, I'll go down to reception and find out how I go about making the call.'

'Tom, why don't you just forget about it, it's a mistake and we can sort it out when we get home? It will cost a fortune to ring home and you may not be any the wiser if you do.'

'Mmm, that's a point, I'll go down and send a telegram to your mother, telling her I will sort it out when we get back, how's that.'

'That is much more sensible.' Tom didn't take the lift he decided to walk down the stairs. He needed time to think, he couldn't understand this, and it was going to mess up the surprise he had planned for Jennifer's birthday. 'Blast, blast, blast,' he said to himself as he walked down the stairs.

What with the time difference and this annoyance with the cheque, Tom didn't sleep at all well. It was eleven o'clock New York time when they awoke. They had breakfast come lunch, and went around to the gallery. It was easy to find, as the man on the desk at the hotel said it would be.

Tom observed, looking at the shops, as they walked, 'This place never stops, it seems as if you could eat anything anytime, night or day, it's incredible.'

'I still wouldn't like to live here, I feel that the place is pushing me, just being here, London's bad enough, but this is worse.'

'Aye, I know what you mean.'

Tom made himself known to the exhibition organiser, Josh Lawrence, a gushing New Yorker, all smiles, and slaps on the back, clearly delighted to meet a "Genuine bona fide English Lady". He was not the sort of person Tom needed when he was tired and annoyed about his cheque bouncing, in addition he was struggling to understand half the fellow said. To exasperate him even further, Jennifer said she was going to walk up Madison Avenue to look at the shops.

'Jen, really I don't think that is wise, I'm not happy about you going out on your own.' Once again, the exuberant Josh jumped in and said, Marilyn from the office would go with her and she would see "The Lady" came to no harm. I'm not going to be able to stand much of this fellow, he's overpowering, and that voice, it's like a finger nail scraping on a blackboard, Tom thought. He was forced to let Jennifer go but the whole deal was turning out to be a nightmare, as far as he was concerned. Once Jennifer had left, Tom asked Josh if he could tell him how to get to the bank. Tom had made arrangements with the help of Reginald Armstrong-Bennett, whilst he was in London, that a bank in New York could access his funds in England. Tom wondered if they might be able to tell him anything. He thought it was a long shot, but he was desperate.

'No, "Prob'" Tommy boy, I'll takes ya there, right now.' Nothing was a problem to Josh, it appeared. He talked incessantly in a nasal accent that had no spaces between the words, and it was wearing Tom out just trying to listen. When they arrived at the bank, the teller was only marginally more understandable. The news was more disturbing; Tom had to ask the man three times to be sure he understood. If he was to understand the man correctly, he only had £150 in his account, but that was all he could tell him.

On the way back to the gallery, Josh was as animated as ever, Tom, didn't even attempt to respond, he was in such a state of confusion, there *must* be some mistake, he said again to himself.

Jennifer had returned by the time he and Josh walked up the stairs into the gallery.

'As soon as my back is turned you are off on the Town, Tom Jackson,' Jennifer said laughing. She quickly changed, when she saw the look on Tom's face, he wasn't looking amused in the slightest.

'Listen Josh, my wife and I have to go back to our hotel, we'll return later.'

'No prob's, Tommy boy, we'll just get on with the unpacking, take as long as you like, you and your Lady.'

'What is it Tom?' Jennifer asked as they walked out.

'I went to the bank, Josh took me, it's near as it happens and they told me, the best I can understand, that I only have £150 in my account.'

'What, that's nonsense, it must be a mistake!'

'But there was the telegram from your mum too, don't forget.'

'Oh I wouldn't worry Tom, we know how much you have. It will be a mix up with it being a new account. In the meantime I'll draw on *my* account so we aren't destitute.'

'Jen, this is no joke.'

'Trust me Tom, it will work out and we will laugh about it later.'

'You think so?' This doesn't solve the problem of Jen's piano he thought.

They didn't go back to the exhibition until the next day; Tom couldn't face the happy, happy of Josh. Josh and his team had unpacked the work by the time Tom and Jennifer arrived the next morning, and to add even more colour to the experience, Tom was informed by Marilyn, that Josh was gay, not that it mattered to him; it was his relentless talking that was grinding Tom to a pulp.

Tom had to admit he was impressed by how these "Yanks" worked, 'Boy, they can teach us English a thing or two, about hard labour, that's for sure,' he said to Jennifer.

In three days the exhibition was set up and ready to open. The pleasure of seeing his work presented actually lightened Tom's mood, much to Jennifer's relief, saying she was pleased to see him smile again.

The next evening the exhibition would be unveiled to the public. There was to be champagne and food laid on for the invited guests.

'Will you *stand still*, Tom,' Jennifer said, as she tied his bow tie, she was feeling his anxiety too.

'I feel ridiculous dressed up like this.' This first evening was to be a black tie "Do" and this would be the first time Tom had worn his new evening suit, or "Tuxedo" as Josh called it.

'As far as I'm concerned, I think you look absolutely wonderful Tom,' Jennifer said, stepping back and admiring his new suit, my aunt was right, 'James Bond 007, in fact I quite fancy you.'

'Ha, ha, very funny, I'm not in the mood, this is stupid.'

'Oh! We are a grump tonight.'

'No I'm not.'

'Ohhh yes you are.'

'Awe... I'm sorry, Jen, I suppose I'm just worked up and anxious, you look fantastic in that frock.

'Whey-man, it's a gown, no a frock,' she said smiling. Tom was compelled to smile too.

'Come here woman, did I tell you I love you?' He said taking her in his arms.

'Actually not in the last couple of days, unless I misheard the grunts.'

'Oh dear, that bad, I'll make it up to you, I'll be the perfect chaperone tonight. How's that?'

'I'll hold you to that.'

'Don't leave me on my own, the place will be full of posh Yanks, and I'll be out of my depth.'

The exhibition had been an undoubted success. Jennifer decided to make up a scrapbook of paper clippings reporting Tom's exhibition. They would read them again on the plane travelling home; it would be a pleasurable way to pass the time on. Jennifer smiled as she passed the cuttings into her book.

"The bar has been raised for new artists": "Artist, Tom Jackson and his glamorous wife Lady Jennifer Jackson wow, New York": "English Artist, the new Monet, paints swallows, in pools of sunlight instead of lilies in pools of water": "Swallow Man, swoops on New York".

'I can't believe the money we have made, I felt as if I just had to think of a number and double it, mad, mad. We still have that business of my money to sort out when we get home, I can't get that clear in my mind.' Tom had his earnings from the exhibition transferred to Jennifer's account, in order to give him some breathing space to resolve the questions back home. He wasn't quite honest with her about how much he had made, because he had arranged, with Josh's help, to transfer money to Reginald Armstrong-Bennett in London. Reginald had kindly offered to organise payment to the piano company in Newcastle, so Jennifer would still get her piano for her birthday.
'You know Jen; this art thing has much to do with confidence and perception. We must be in no doubt the debt we owe Reginald, it is down to a string of circumstances that we are where we are now.'
'I still believe your work is exceptional, Tom.'

'Supposing it is. Right now, somewhere there is a guy every bit as good as me, struggling to get anyone to even look at his work. That is the truth of it; perhaps my work is good, I really don't know. For me, painting is simply a release of something inside, and by the grace of God, Reginald was led to my exhibition in Newcastle. Just as surely as I thank God that at a given moment in time I was sitting on a bench by the sea.'

'When you put it like that it is all frightfully amazing,' she said and kissed him.

'Before we return to the North East I want to go and see Reginald and personally thank him, he is such a kind man.'

Chapter Twenty-Two

The flight home was to be a seriously different experience to the one on the way out to America. This flight was to provide maximum entertainment for all, especially those new to the joys of flying, such as Jennifer and Tom.

Once the flight was on its way, their plan to relax and read their newspaper reviews never entered their heads. There were high winds and excessive turbulence for most of the journey home. The plane felt to drop thousands of feet suddenly. Neither Tom nor Jennifer spoke as it went through the squalls. They were both frightened, as were most of the other passengers. Children were crying, and occasionally an adult lost their composure and screamed.

The person next to Jennifer was violently sick and *not* in the bag provided. They had to get out of their seat and try to balance in the aisle as the stewardess had the unenviable task of cleaning up the mess, which was everywhere including on Jennifer. Jennifer was struggling with sickness as it was, due to her pregnancy, without the smell of someone else's vomit drifting up her nose. Once the mess had been cleaned up, the poor woman sat groaning and moaning for the rest of the journey with her head in a bag. Tom swapped places with Jennifer so that she might have *some* distance from the acrid smell, but he was still expecting her to be sick any minute.

It was worse on take-off and landing, everyone breathed a sigh of relief when they were walking down the steps of the plane in London, even if the rain was torrential. Tom imagined that the pilots would be just as pleased as the passengers that this nightmare flight was over.

They stayed in London for two days and visited Reginald at the gallery. He was delighted to see them. He had heard from the gallery in New York and beamed with pleasure.

'Am I or am I not a great judge of art, Tom?' He laughed, 'The talk of New York I hear.'

'From my point of view, it all went without a hitch, Reginald. I owe you more than words can say.'

'In my world money speaks my boy and my company are the richer for meeting you. I have not done too badly myself, from my bonuses, *and* my prestige in the art world has shot up. So, it is *we*, who are in your debt.

May I also say, it's good to see you looking so well, my Lady, and congratulations on the news of the expected addition to your family.'

'Thank you, Reginald, we have had a splendid time, apart from the flight home, what a frightful experience that was.'

As they were leaving, Reginald tugged Tom's sleeve, winked and nodded, which Tom understood to mean that he had attended to the birthday present for Jennifer. They shook hands and said they were looking forward to meeting again.

'I will be in touch Tom, this is not the end of our association, but the beginning.'

'Jennifer and I are going to spend some quiet time together, some "Jennifer and Tom time", probably up at our house by the coast, this has been a whirlwind of a period in our lives. I may even do a little painting.'

'Whatever you do, don't forget me, I'm only a phone call away remember.' Reginald walked them to the entrance of the gallery and shook hands, wishing them well. 'Bless you both, safe journey.'

Jennifer and Tom were exhausted by the time they arrived at Newcastle station. They took a taxi home to the Lodge where they lived. Tom had to wake Jennifer, in the half hour drive from the station she had slumped against him, fast asleep.'

'We're home Jen,' Tom said, gently stroking her cheek.

She opened her eyes, but it took her a moment to wake, Tom kissed her head.

'Mmm,' she said stretching, 'I could sleep for a week, Tom.'

'We will. First, let's get out of the taxi,' she smiled. Their luggage, along with the presents they had bought for their families was set down at the house door, while Tom paid the taxi driver.

'Come on Tom, you have the key let's get inside. I hope mummy's put some milk in the fridge, I could murder a cup of tea.'

'Not so fast.'

'Pardon?'

'Do you know what today is?'

'Sorry, what do you mean, I'm not with you?'

'This is a very *extraordinary* day, it's my beautiful wife's birthday.'

'Tom, I thought you had forgotten.' Jennifer said smiling, 'what exactly do you mean?' Jennifer's emotions were now somewhere between uncontrollable excitement and fear and foreboding.

'You have done something, what is it, tell me, tell me?'

'I can't believe you would think that I would forget such an important occasion. Let's go inside and see what the *fairies* have brought.' He put the key in the lock then withdrew it, 'On second thoughts, this can wait, perhaps we should go and see your mum and dad first.'

'Tom! You are wicked, open this door, this instant.'

'Temper, temper, okay, close your eyes.' Tom unlocked the door, he hoped that this was not going to be a big disappointment, thinking this will be a *giant* "None event" if the piano isn't here. He pushed open the lounge door and there it was, in front of the bay window, with a large red ribbon wrapped around it.

'Are you ready, no peeping Jen. Are you *really* sure you want to see it?'

'Tom, will you stop teasing, you're killing me.'

'Right, you can look now.' She nervously removed her hands from her eyes and was completely silent. She only stood and stared with her mouth open and then collapsed into an armchair.

'Tom,' she began to cry, 'Tom, I can't believe this. No one has ever done anything like this for me.' Tom knelt down and took her in his arms. Her tears ran down his face as well as hers. 'Tom, you are the kindest person, it must have cost a fortune.'

'Paid for, courtesy of New York's finest.'

'There are no words to tell you how I love you, not because of the money, but to think that you would go to all this trouble, just for me, to make me feel so special.'

'But you *are* special. Come on it's not just to look at, play me a tune. You'll need to play all the time; I couldn't afford a radio too. It was either the piano or radio so I went for the piano. Come on, take that ribbon off and open your present.'

Tom stood and gently pulled Jennifer to her feet. She loosened the red ribbon and ran her hand over the polished surface.

'It's beautiful Tom, I'm almost afraid to touch it.' She sat at the stool, adjusted its height, and lifted the fallboard exposing the gleaming white keys.

'We should really raise the lid.'

'At your service, maestro.' Tom lifted the lid carefully and fitted the support in place to hold it up.

'I have no music, Tom.'

'Play the tune you played in London, remember, you impressed John Lennon and everyone else. They stopped looking at my pictures, recognising real art.' She smiled, sat quietly for a moment then raised her hands from her lap and began to play. Every note was crystal clear; they seemed to float and dance on the air. She didn't play the piece she had played in London; instead, she played Brahms' Lullaby.

Tom lowered himself quietly down into an armchair, he was choking this was torture. This moment was a memory that he knew was being burned permanently into his brain, with a red-hot iron. He tried to swallow and pushed his knuckle against his lips, in an attempt to compose himself. She was silhouetted by the sunlight streaming through the window. It sparkled on her hair and touched the edges of her face. Her classical beauty was accentuated by the light; he was now gripping the arms of the chair. Fortunately, she was lost in the magic of her playing and didn't notice the torment he was going through.

Jennifer finished the piece, and rested her hands on her lap and bowed her head.

'That was a prayer,' she whispered, 'I played it for our baby... I know I'm being silly, but I wanted our baby to be part of this once in a lifetime moment.' Then Jennifer quietly turned to him, and she could see how moved he was.

'Please don't be sad, Tom,' she knew what he was thinking. She came to him, sat on his knee, and pressed her lips to his forehead. They quietly held each other.

Eventually, Jennifer broke the silence, 'Thank you, Tom, for all the trouble you have gone to for *me.*'

It was some time before they were able to move. They were two people simply loving each other. Tom removed his handkerchief from his pocket and wiped his face.

'Boy, oh, boy, this is tough; it's me who thanks you, Jen. I must freshen up and then we ought to bring in our cases, they are still standing at the front door. Unless they have been pinched,' Tom tried to joke, Jennifer smiled and kissed him.

'Come on then, let me help you up, and we'll go and see mummy and daddy.'

Chapter Twenty-Three

As they made their way up to her mother and father's house, Jennifer asked Tom if her mother was engaged in this deception with the piano.

'Jen, you have no idea, that was why I was so concerned about the telegram your mum sent to me in New York. She was my contact while we were away, the firm was to liaise with your mum, she has been an absolute star.'

'Ah, I see.'

'I will have to go to the bank tomorrow to clear that up, it was a flipping pest, your mum must have felt foolish, how embarrassing for her. I will have to apologise to her, your dad's not going to be pleased, that I do know. I only hope he has had a good day at the office and is feeling generous towards me. It was Reginald who finally came up with the goods.'

'Reginald *knew* too?'

'Yes, and good old Josh, you *can't* imagine, it's been an international effort.'

'*Never*, I appreciate everyone's kindness; you have given me the best present ever. I don't know how you could possibly top that.'

'Mmm,' was all Tom said, *this* is one of the triggers I have to avoid, he thought, or I will be plunged into that pit of despair, which is always just a step away. There may *never* be another birthday, went through his mind.

'I enjoyed it too, your face was a picture,' he quickly replied, before he had time to dwell on gloomier things, and he tried to smile.

'It's odd, I thought mummy would have been out to meet us, they knew when we were arriving. I would imagine reports of our taxi have reached her ears by now.'

They walked in, and Jennifer called out, 'Mummy, Daddy, we're home.' Her mother came into the hallway.

'*Jennifer!*'

'Are you all right Mummy, you look frightful?' Jennifer's joy was immediately changed into concern.

'Oh, Jennifer darling, Tom, it's awful, terrible,' she looked at them almost pleading and then she slumped against the wall, with her face in her hands. Tom and Jennifer immediately went to support her.

'Come on Mummy, whatever is it? Let's go into the room and sit down. You can tell us what's happened, is it, daddy?' Tom and

Jennifer helped her mother into the sitting room and sat down with her on the settee.

'Take your time Mummy, and tell us what has happened, is daddy all right, has something happened to him?' She asked again.

'Tom, how will you ever forgive us?' Lady Carolyn's face was one of desperation.

'Whatever is it Mummy, what do you mean, forgive you?'

'Your father has stolen all Tom's money, it's all gone.' Tom and Jennifer's faces were utterly blank. They were speechless.

'But Mummy, I don't understand, what do you mean?'

'Jeremy Henderson set up some spurious company in Rhodesia and encouraged your father to invest heavily, with promises of a fortune. He borrowed against the estate and Jeremy has run off with all the money. The bank wanted their money from your father, they must have got wind of his predicament, and your father took Tom's. Forgive us Tom, but Peter would have lost everything, he was desperate and apparently Tom, you had signed the executive power to Peter, which gave him access to your account. I didn't know anything about it, he has only just told me this afternoon. We will pay it all back somehow, every penny, I promise.'

Tom was still speechless.

'Where is Daddy now?'

'He went out when he saw you arrive in the taxi, he couldn't face Tom after the way he looked down on him.'

Tom stood up abruptly and smacked his fist into the palm of his hand.

'Tom!' Jennifer pleaded.

'It's not your father that makes my blood boil, it's that low life, Jeremy Henderson, I will strangle him if I get my hands on him.'

'Where is he?'

'No one knows, his mother and father have gone to Rhodesia, to see if they can find him. Apparently, many people have lost money. What about Peter, how will you ever forgive him?'

'Look, this place will belong to our baby one day, so what, if it has cost me to keep it, I don't care a fig about the money.'

'Thank you, Tom,' Jennifer said.

'Peter will never be able to face you, Tom.'

'He went out the back of the house, you said.'

'Yes, I have asked Warwick to go and find him, he can't run away.'

'Look, I'll go out and put his mind at rest. Don't worry yourself; I would have probably done the same thing. I would have given it to him if he had asked. So there is no problem, not with Lord Peter anyway, he doesn't need to apologise. You stay here with your mum Jen, get her some sweet tea.' With that, Tom went out to the rear of the house and began to look around the stable block; he saw Warwick and two other fellows coming from the kitchen gardens.

'Ah, Mr Warwick, have you seen anything.'

'No Sir.'

'Where have you looked?'

'Nowhere yet Sir, I went first to the gardens to get Phil and Jimmy to help.'

'Good idea, I'll continue to look around these buildings here; you three spread out and search the grounds, you have got to have a better idea where to look than me. No need to disturb him if you see him, just come and tell me where he is.'

'Very good, Sir.' They walked off, and Tom continued searching the stables and outbuildings. He tugged at the stiff garage door where Jennifer kept her car, but it wouldn't budge. When he looked carefully, he could just see through the joint of the door that it was bolted on the inside.

'Oh hell,' he frantically tugged again at the door, but it wouldn't budge. He looked around to see if there was some other way in and noticed a small window further along the wall. He went to it and wiped it with his sleeve. By the look of the grime, it hadn't been cleaned for years. He pressed his face to the glass, shaded his eyes, and squinted through the dirt, attempting to look inside.

'Oh, dear God,' he could just see in, it was dark, but he could make out a rope and a body catching what light there was, as it swayed and turned slightly under its weight. He anxiously looked around for something to break the glass with. There was a pile of logs stacked against the wall near where he was standing. He reached down, took one and smashed the glass, then laid his jacket over the bottom of the window frame to protect himself as he climbed in. It was a tight squeeze, and he had to wriggle to get through. He gave a final push with his foot and dropped to the ground, falling onto the shards of broken glass. Quickly getting up he went to the door, flipped the bolt, and dragged the door open; glancing at his hands and arm, as he tugged at the door he saw the blood. It was gushing from the cuts and dripping off his fingers. His side had been cut too as he pushed through the small opening and the blood was soaking into his shirt, but he ignored it, he didn't seem to be in any pain. He turned and went quickly to Jennifer's father. Tom tried to lift him by his legs to relieve the pressure on his neck but was unable to, and he cried out in frustration. He looked for something to cut the rope with but couldn't see anything. Dashing to the door he yelled for Warwick, after a few minutes of Tom's bellowing, Mr Warwick came running across the yard towards him, followed by Phil and Jimmy.

'What's happened to you Sir, you're covered in blood?'

'Never mind me, in here, quick, I can't manage.' Warwick stopped in his tracks when he saw Lord Peter. He was apparently horrified at the sight before him.

'Quick man don't just stand there. Help me lift him. One of you drag that bench over here, jump up and take the rope off his neck while we lift, come on, come on, as quick as you can.'

Together, Warwick and Tom lifted Lord Peter, Phil steadied the small table while Jimmy climbed on it and removed the noose from his Lordship's neck.

'Flipping heck, he weighs a ton, careful, easy does it.'

They gently laid Lord Peter on the ground and Tom attempted to give him artificial respiration. He had been one of the first-aiders at the school where he had taught, so he knew what to do, in theory.

'Quick Warwick, go and ring for an ambulance, can you do it without Lady Carolyn knowing?'

'Yes Sir, I'll ring from the kitchen.'

'Right, do that, then wait at the front of the house to show them where we are, when they arrive.' Tom held Lord Peter's nose and breathed into his mouth, Lord Peter's chest rose and fell. He repeated the procedure several times, but there was no sign of life. Tom felt dizzy and fell back.

'Are you all right, Sir, you are bleeding badly.' Tom took a moment to reply.

'Yes, but you're right, I will have to see to these cuts.' He tried to stand but stumbled, and Phil caught him by the arm.

'You'd better let me help you, Sir.'

'Just give me a minute to pull myself together, I'll be all right.'

'It's no good Sir... he's dead.'

'What! No he can't be, let me try again,' Tom tried, and then shook his head in despair and sat back, his head was spinning.

'Stay here until Warwick comes back, I'll go in speak to Lady Carolyn.' Tom staggered back to the house and leant against the doorframe to gain as much strength as he could before he went in. He looked at his hands; the cuts were on fire now. He stumbled into the room, when Jennifer saw him, she screamed. All she could see was that he was covered in blood, his shirt was saturated down his left side, and it was dripping from his hands. Tom was unable to stand any longer and fell forward onto his knees.

'Quick Mummy, ring for an ambulance.'

'No need, no need, there's one on its way,' Tom gasped.

'Have you got something for a tourniquet, Mummy, and cloth for bandages, quickly, ring for Beth; we need water and disinfectant too. Jennifer decided she couldn't wait for Beth to bring the cloth and tugged a cloth from a table, a vase of flowers tumbled to the ground smashing as it hit the floor. She tore the cloth and twisted it around Tom's arm to stop the bleeding, which was severe, especially from his right wrist. There were pieces of glass in Tom's hands too. Jennifer tried to pick out the pieces that were obvious. She noticed that she had cut her finger in the process, which she dabbed on a piece of cloth. When she was satisfied, she held him while she waited for Beth. Once Beth had brought water and bandages Jennifer washed Tom's wounds and bandaged them the best she was able. Tom groaned several times but never spoke. It was not until she had done all she could, did she ask Tom again, to tell her what had happened.

'Thanks Beth, you can go and get yourself washed,' Tom managed to say. She looked towards Lady Carolyn.

'Yes, you go, thank you, Beth.' Tom waited until Beth had closed the door.

'Help me up,' they both helped Tom, and he sat on a chair at a table. 'Sit down both of you.'

'What is it Tom?' Tom only managed to give them the bare-bones of the story.

Seeing Jennifer holding Lady Carolyn in her arms was the last thing he could recall.

Chapter Twenty-Four

The next thing he knew, he was in the hospital, with a drip in his arm and Jennifer sitting by his bed. Tom looked up at the drip, then to Jennifer.

'Hello you,' he said.

'Hello, Tom.' Jennifer just stared at him and took his bandaged hand as he reached out to her.

'I'm sorry Jennifer, I tried I really did, honestly.'

'I know, Warwick told us how you gave Daddy artificial respiration. He said you gave him the kiss of life several times and all the time you were bleeding to death.'

'I think that may be a touch overdramatic.'

'No, I was frightened Tom, really frightened, I could see the look on the ambulance men's faces, they were worried too. You were frightfully pale. Having lost so much blood, we feared you were going to die,' she bowed her head.

'I don't remember any of this,' he nodded to the drip.

'No, you were unconscious when we brought you in, I was terrified.'

'If only I had been quicker, Jen, only a couple of minutes and I might have been able to save him.' He tensed and groaned.

'Careful Tom, they had to operate on your side, try to keep still. They said one of your kidneys was cut by the glass, it was that serious.'

'Ahhh, flipping heck,' he groaned again as he relaxed back into his pillow. 'What about your mum?'

'Aunty Susan, mummy's sister, is with her. She has been ever so kind. My cousin Louise has been too, we went for a long walk together, we have been friends since we were children. She has always been full of fun. She didn't say much, we merely walked, it's good to have someone, one can just be with, without the pressure of having to talk.'

'I'm glad, how long have I been here, it's all a bit of a haze. I'm sure, I have woken a time or two, but I can't remember.'

'The doctors sedated you. They were awfully kind. You have been here for three days now. The nurse said it can take a while before the anaesthetic wears off, so don't be surprised if you feel a trifle odd at times.'

'Ah, I feel as if I have been sucking an old sock, I have the most ghastly taste in my mouth.'

'I have brought you some juice in, let me get you a drink,' Jennifer poured him some juice into a glass on the bedside cabinet. Tom raised himself, and Jennifer supported his head, while she touched the glass to his lips and he sipped a little from it.'

Again he groaned as he lay back into the pillows, 'Ahhh, thanks Jen, I needed that, not that I'm really thirsty, it's just the horrid taste in my mouth.'

'I have some mints in my bag, would you like one of those?'

'Yes, I will have one, thanks,' Jennifer passed one to him.

'I have missed you, Tom. I needed you. It helped to hold your hand.'

'Surely you've not been sitting here all the time.'

'Most of the time, when they would let me, as I said, the staff have been very kind. Doctor Hart even came to see you; she had seen you being brought in. We sat and talked, that was a surprise, what a special lady she is, more like a friend.'

'How much longer do I have to stay in here?'

'They think until the end of the week. The doctor said he couldn't believe all that you had done when the ambulance men gave their report.'

'Honestly, I am struggling to remember any details. They probably exaggerated.'

'Your wounds weren't an exaggeration.' He glanced again at the bandages on his hands. 'Are you in much pain?' Jennifer asked.

'A little, not much, unless I move it seems.'

Jennifer told him what had been happening since he came into the hospital. The ambulance men had called for a doctor to certify the death and *he* said that the police had to be informed.

'It was absolutely frightful, Tom.' They hadn't been allowed to move Lord Peter's body until the police had completed their investigation. They interviewed everyone; it appeared that Tom's input wasn't required at this time, but it was possible that a coroner might call him.

'They seemed satisfied that daddy had committed...' Jennifer bowed her head. There had been reporters waiting outside the gates, even television cameras.

'They were all like vultures Tom, not the slightest concern for our grief and how we might be feeling, wanting to know all the gruesome details of the death. Aunt Susan has been wonderful, she spoke to them.'

Eventually, the police said that they would not be pursuing the case, in their opinion, it was a suicide, and they would send their report to the Coroner in due course.

Tom stayed in the hospital for one more day then he discharged himself and ordered a taxi to pick him up at the hospital and take him home. He thought the taxi journey was never going to end, every bump in the road shot pain through his side.

Jennifer was startled when he walked in; she was sitting with her Aunt, Susan.

'Tom, *what* are you doing here, they said you would be in the hospital for at least two more days!'

'They needed the bed.'

'Tom, you're lying.'

'Just a little, they were busy, anyway I needed to get back here.'

'Hello, Mr Bond.' Jennifer's aunt said smiling and reached over and gently held Tom's bandaged hand.

'Hello Aunt Susan, is that what I should call you, I'm never quite sure?'

'That's fine by me, but Miss Moneypenny will do just as well.' Tom smiled, 'I'm trying to joke, but really, I don't feel remotely like laughing, I am quite devastated as we all are.'

'It was so unnecessary if I had only been quicker a few seconds might have made the difference.'

'You can't blame yourself, Tom. Are you in much pain?'

'Not too bad really, a bit sore that's all. I'm glad to be out of that hospital.'

'Jennifer told me you received some dreadful cuts and lost a great deal of blood. We are terribly grateful, for all you've done, you could have died yourself. By all accounts, your effort was quite heroic.'

'I can't honestly tell you about that. Jen has *told me* how sportive *you* have been, especially to her mum.'

'That's what families do, isn't it?'

Jennifer sent for another cup and told Tom what had been happening since they last spoke.

'Any news about that swine Henderson?'

'No, I've not heard anything.'

He's not getting away with this.'

Tom asked if he could see Jennifer's mum. 'Will you bring my cup of tea, I'll drink it with your mum?' Jennifer took Tom upstairs to her mother's room. She knocked on her mother's bedroom door, waited a moment, and then went in. Her mother was sitting by her bedroom window staring out across the parkland. She turned as Tom and Jennifer entered, and then hung her head. Tom walked over and sat opposite her. He reached out and took her hand between his bandaged hands.

'Your poor hands Tom, you had beautiful fine hands, you must hate us,' Lady Carolyn said staring at the bandages.

'Must I! What for, we have all suffered, you most of all, no I don't hate you, you are my family, and we are all hurting together.'

'You are a kind man Tom. Jennifer is fortunate to have found you. I could not have wished for a better son-in-law.'

'I think it's me who is the lucky one. Would you do something for me, Lady Carolyn?'

'What can I do, I feel useless?'

'Take me for a walk; I have been cooped up for days in that hospital, now I need some fresh air. We can walk in the wood at the back of the house it's quite private. Would you do that?'

'Oh I don't know Tom,' she looked up at Jennifer who was now standing behind Tom with her hands resting on his shoulders.'

'It's no good looking at Jennifer, it would be a kindness to me.'

'Go on Mummy, it would do you both good.'

'Hmm, if you think so Jennifer, I am so frightfully tired. Perhaps a walk will wake me up.' With that, Lady Carolyn eased herself up from her chair, went to the wardrobe, and took out her overcoat and a headscarf.

They went downstairs, and Jennifer left them to walk on their own. She stood at the door as they walked off. Lady Carolyn had her arm through Tom's. Jennifer smiled nodding as she watched them go.

'Mother's right Tom, you *are* a kind man, I am so fortunate that you love me,' she said to herself.

Tom asked Lady Carolyn questions about the park and the various trees as they strolled along the path, which twisted its way through the wood. The track had clearly been designed to create a pleasant walk and show off the area to its best. Tom also asked about Jennifer, he was glad to hear anything about her, and Lady Carolyn seemed pleased to tell him. She relaxed as they talked and she even smiled once or twice at her recollections. Carolyn cried a little when she spoke of Lord Peter, but Tom ignored it. She told him how she and Lord Peter had first met on holiday in Venice. He had thought she was Italian and she had thought he was, they were both too shy to speak. They had been staying in the same hotel with their respective parents.

'We kept glancing at each other across the dining room at meal times. I was only eighteen; it was love at first sight. How we laughed when we discovered that we both came from Northumberland,' she told Tom, and he smiled.

'Life, when one is young, is all to be lived, Tom. One never imagines there will be any problems, awful things happen to *other* people, don't they?'

Carolyn said all her memories had come flooding back to her when Jennifer told her how she had met Tom. She told him that it was clear to her how much Jennifer loved him; she could see Jennifer come to life when she was near him, and she remembered that feeling.

'Will you be my friend, Tom?' Lady Carolyn asked him.

'I think we are already friends Carolyn, but I'm never going to get away with "Bunny".' She smiled up at him, drew him down to her, and kissed him.

'This is so hard, Tom.'

'Yes, it is. Losing someone you really love has got to be as bad as it gets. I think we will need each other, Carolyn.' Tom remembered John Lennon saying to him when they had met in London, *"You don't know what pain is till you lose someone you really love"*. Those words had stuck in his head like glue.

'Do you believe in God, Tom?'

'I honestly don't know what I believe, Carolyn. I have never gone to church, but I have been praying lately, as you can imagine I have fears, *and* it really has made me feel better. Make of that what you will.'

'Do you think if there is a God, He could ever forgive Peter?'

'My dear Carolyn, *I* would give anything to have Peter here with us, if that amounts to forgiveness, I'm pretty sure God has a greater capacity to forgive than I do. If He does not, then there is no hope for any of us.'

'I forgive him too, Tom, so I will take comfort in what you say.' Tom turned her to him and hugged her.

Jennifer and her Aunt Susan were sitting when Tom and Lady Carolyn walked into the lounge, and they politely stood.

'What's it like to walk out with James Bond, Carolyn?' Asked her sister, Susan, Carolyn looked puzzled.

'Aunty Susan thinks Tom looks like a film star, Mummy, who plays a British secret agent, called James Bond.'

Carolyn looked at Tom. 'I've heard of him, do you know, he does; now you mention it. I knew there was something familiar about you when I first saw you, Tom. Of course, I see it now.'

'Alright, can we drop this please, three onto one's not fair,' Tom said blushing.

At that point Louise came in, 'What are you all smiling at?'

'Don't any of you dare,' said Tom. 'Remember, I'm a sick man, and should be looked after.' Jennifer came to Tom, and wrapped her arms around his neck and kissed him.

'Awe, my poor Darling, I will look after you, let me bathe your brow.'

'Okay, okay don't over do it, now you're taking the Michael, and I can't beat you because of my hands.' Jennifer smiled at him and kissed him again.

The following weeks continued to be very difficult. After the funeral, which was a quiet family affair, apart from all the photographers, whom they did their best to ignore, Tom and Jennifer took Lady Carolyn with them up to the quiet village by the sea, where Tom's house was.

They stayed at the pub where they had had their first drink. Tom didn't feel he could subject Carolyn *or* Jennifer to the harsh regime of living at his rented house; it was perhaps just *too* basic.

Tom sought out the owner of the three cottages and offered to buy them. The current owner seemed more than willing to sell them. A price was agreed, and Tom decided that as soon as the contract was signed, he would organise for plans to be drawn up and the cottages renovated.

Jennifer's mother was relieved to have this quiet time. There were times when they all walked on the beach together, and there were times when Lady Carolyn left them, and walked alone with her thoughts, allowing the wind and salt air to work their magic and bring some healing.

Tom recalled how *he* had walked along the beach, exactly as Jennifer's mother was now doing, not *too* many months past. This time together by the sea had been an invaluable bonding time, for which Tom was thankful.

Chapter Twenty-Five

'I've got it, Jen,' Tom called and picked up the telephone receiver. 'Hello, Gosforth 2809, Tom Jackson speaking.' It was Tom's architect, who was drawing the plans for the alterations to the cottages by the sea.

'Mr Jackson, it's John Sanderson here, we have the draft plans ready for your perusal, do you want me to pop them in the post, or do you want to come to the office?'

'Excellent, this is quicker than I hoped for. We'll come to the office, and then we can discuss what's what, face to face. If you send them, it will take longer, and I want this finished as soon as possible.'

'Great, that suits us. When shall we say? Are you able to come this afternoon, how about 1:30?'

'Hang on a sec',' Tom called to Jennifer, 'Jen have we anything on today at 1:30?'

'No, nothing,' he heard Jennifer reply.

'That's perfect, Mr Sanderson, we'll see you then.' Tom hung up.

'That was the architect, Jen,' he told her as she came into the hallway. 'I said we would go to see the plans this afternoon at 1:30. I know you are better in the afternoon and I want you to have your input so that I'm sure what we are seeing on the plans, is how we both imagined it to be.'

'How thrilling, I can't wait to see them, Tom.'

Jennifer was struggling now; her bump was growing and causing pains in her back and hips. She wouldn't take medication for the pain because of her fear of causing any distress or endangering their baby's health. Jennifer was due to see Doctor Hart the following week. Tom hoped that Doctor Hart would be, *one,* able to prescribe some medication, and *two,* convince Jennifer that there would not be any risk to their baby if she took it.

Fortunately, Tom was able to drive the car now, thanks to Jennifer's foresight, which took all that responsibility for transport off her shoulders. Jennifer found it difficult at the beginning when he drove and made sure she got to the car before him and into the driver's seat. Little by little, Tom had made his way behind the wheel, and Jennifer grew in confidence. She was now forced to concede that he was, in fact, an excellent driver. She did wonder if his first horrific moments in control of the car, or more accurately, "*Not* in control of the car", and the memory of that World War Two air raid shelter looming towards them had scarred him for life. She knew for sure, she would never be teaching another learner driver after that experience. She smiled, thinking that perhaps it was just that he was concerned for her and his pending family. Whatever the reason he was an extremely careful driver, and she felt confident when he drove, which she *never* thought she would.

'I'm really excited Jen, it will be wonderful to have that property renovated, nowhere will ever replace that house in my heart. Suppose that in the future we have other houses, that house, will always be my home. We will be able to go up any time we wish at a moments notice, it only takes an hour and a bit to get there.'

'I love the place too Tom, and of course, it will be a great place to bring up our baby. It's safe, and I like the people. It will be good for mummy too, although she is ever conscious of our needs, and fears she is intruding,'

'That's nonsense, she would never do that, I will talk to her. She could do with moving out of that big house and finding somewhere smaller, she literally rattles around in there.'

'We both know that is never going to happen, but if we can talk her into coming up there with us occasionally, that will ease her loneliness.'

'I will speak to her as soon as the house is finished, I know she likes it up there.'

Tom tapped his fingers on the steering wheel in frustration, as he waited for the traffic lights to change. He glanced at his watch concerned that they were going to be late for their appointment.

'Gosh, it's busy today, the traffic is heavy, will you drop me at John Sanderson's office Tom, so I don't have to walk? Then you can go and park the car.'

'Of course, I will, I intended to do that anyway.' Tom turned up a side street next to John Sanderson's office and stopped behind a big black Mercedes. Leaving the engine running he jumped out and dashed around to open the car door for Jennifer, took her arm, helping her out. They were on double yellow lines but this was only going to take a second, and it didn't seem to be worrying the owner of the Mercedes, thought Tom and smiled. The Vitesse was quite low, and it was a little awkward for Jennifer to get out, because of the pains in her back, they were severely limiting her mobility now.

'You go into the office Jen, tell them I'll be there as soon as I have parked the car. I'll only be five minutes, there is a big car park just down the bottom of the street, on the other side of the junction,' he said nodding his head in the direction of the car park. As he helped Jennifer out of the car, he could see she was in considerable pain; she was biting her lip to prevent herself calling out. Tom gave her a quick kiss, jumped back into the car, waved, and was just about to pull out, when the driver of the Mercedes came from the building next to the car, opened the boot of the Mercedes and dropped in a brown holdall.

Tom couldn't believe his eyes, it was *Jeremy Henderson* as large as life. Tom slammed on the brakes; the Vitesse was now diagonally across the road. He leapt out leaving the door wide open; Jeremy looked up and immediately saw Tom. Jeremy grabbed Jennifer who had her back to him at that moment. She was watching Tom and never noticed him. Jeremy held her with one of his arms around her neck and with his other hand; he twisted her arm up her back. She screamed as her back twisted.

'Don't come any closer or I'll break her neck, it won't be the first time, there were loads of Niggers to practice on in Rhodesia.' Tom was in the eye of the hurricane and yet he had never felt so calm in the whole of his life. Jennifer couldn't struggle, her knees gave way, and she slumped down, causing the pressure on her neck to increase. She was losing consciousness, her head was spinning, Tom could see that, but he never flinched.

'You are in my world now, *Henderson* and you are hurting my wife, that means you are going to feel pain like you never imagined, *do you* understand?' The iced tone of Tom's words drove them into Jeremy's brain, like shards of surgical steel, Jeremy began to tremble, and there were beads of sweat forming on his brow. Tom's gaze never wavered from Jeremy's eyes; his expression was almost completely frozen apart from a slight flexing of his jaw muscles. The only movement was his gaze, which followed every move and burned into Jeremy. Jeremy continued to hold Jennifer by the throat as he worked his way to the driver's door of his Mercedes. She had stopped struggling and screaming now, overcome by her debilitating pain. A policeman must have heard the disturbance and was now running up the street towards them. Tom had his back to him; his eyes never left Jeremy's. Jeremy looked past Tom and saw the policeman coming. He pushed Jennifer towards Tom and leapt into his car.

'I'm alright Tom, I'm alright,' she gasped and stumbled into his arms. In his panic, Jeremy couldn't get the car started. Tom sat Jennifer on the pavement just as the policeman was arriving.

'Hoy, what's gannin on here!' the policeman shouted drawing his truncheon, 'Stand where ya are.' Tom ignored him and went to the driver's door pulling on the handle, but it was locked. The Mercedes started, Jeremy revved the engine and tore off. The sudden movement and the friction of his clothes against the car spun Tom around, and his hand grabbed the open boot as the car past him. He clung on to the bottom edge of the boot and was dragged about fifty yards to the junction. Jeremy paused briefly at the intersection, just a moment but it was long enough for Tom to swing his left leg up and into the boot. As Jeremy sped away from the scene, Tom dragged himself fully into the boot. The lid was bouncing up and down and struck his ankle as he was clambering in, but he didn't feel a thing, adrenaline was surging through his body and numbing any pain.

Jeremy was driving like a madman, and as he sped in and out through the traffic, Tom was thrown from side to side in the boot. He wrapped his arms around his head to give him some protection as he bounced against the sides of the car.

After about ten minutes of this, he could see that they were clear of the town now, the car was slowing, 'He's pulling into a lay-by to close the boot,' Tom said to himself. He was right; the car swung off the main carriageway and came abruptly to a standstill. Tom quickly clambered out keeping as low as he could, and then crouched down out of sight. Sure enough, Jeremy came around to the rear of the car, at which point Tom stood up. Jeremy stepped back, and his mouth fell open, his eyes bulged, he was stunned to see Tom.

'But how, where have *you* come from!'

'It's *magic*, and for my next trick, I'm going to make *you* disappear, for good.' Jeremy lunged for Tom but stumbled on the roadside curb. Tom stepped to one side as Jeremy grasped for him, all in the same movement, he brought his knee up under Jeremy's chin as he fell forward and then kicked him in the stomach as he tumbled to the ground. Jeremy lay on the road groaning.

'Too slow, not so amazing now, are you? You need to be quicker than that, but you're used to hurting women, a bit different taking someone on your own size.'

This was one plus to having been brought up in Waterloo Terrace, you knew how to take care of yourself, poor Jeremy hadn't a hope. Blood and saliva were pouring from Jeremy's lips now, he gurgled and moaned, gasping for breath as he attempted to spit out a broken tooth. Tom kicked him again, grabbed him by the coat collar, and dragged him to the edge of the lay-by. There was a big articulated lorry hurtling down the dual carriageway towards them, flashing his lights, he couldn't pull over he was going to hit them. Tom pressed Jeremy's head onto the road, so he faced the oncoming lorry. Are you ready to meet your maker, *you jerk*?'

'No 'lease, 'lease don't, I'll p-ay you 'ack,' he begged, screaming and mumbling out the garbled words in a shower of blood and saliva, spraying from his distorted jaw, which was clearly broken.

'Ah, you're not worth it,' Tom snarled pulling him back off the road by the "Scruff of his neck", dropping him and kicking him once again, he was beaten. He had even wet himself; he was utterly at Tom's mercy. 'You're just not worth it,' Tom repeated in disgust. 'I have something to live for. Hell in the form of prison is waiting to welcome you, and God help you, once you're in there, they will love your type. Perhaps I can get a ticket to watch your initiation. I feel dirty just being near you.' The articulated lorry roared passed them with the driver honking his horn at them, it passed only feet from Jeremy's head, enveloping them in a cloud of fumes and dust, he screamed again, but couldn't move because Tom had his foot on his neck, pressing his face painfully onto the gravel. When the dust cleared, Tom could just make out the flashing lights of a police patrol car, which had pulled into the lay-by behind them, its siren blaring, and two policemen jumped out and came towards him.

'Stand well back, turn around and place your hands on the back of the car.'

'NO, officer!' he heard Jennifer's voice and saw her struggling out of the back of the police car, 'That's my husband.' The policeman turned back to Jennifer and watched her go to Tom's side, Tom held her.

'You take your wife to the police car, Sir and sit in the rear seat, your wife's a bit shaken up, and you don't look too good either.'

Tom looked down at himself his clothes were torn, he had lost a shoe, and there was blood soaking into his trouser leg. 'We'll see to this now, we'll have to radio for some assistance, do you need an ambulance?'

'Yes, he does officer, he is badly cut on his leg and his knee.'

'Right, I'll see to that, just sit in the car, as I said. I suppose he'll need an ambulance anyway,' the Policeman pointed to Jeremy.

Tom helped Jennifer into the car then climbed in after her. Jennifer leant into Tom, and he held her, she was shaking.

'Thank God you are safe, I thought you would be killed when his car roared off, your leg was bumping along the road.'

'It probably looks worse than it is.' Tom tried to make light of it for Jennifer's sake, but he was in pain now, the skin had been torn from his knee as he was dragged behind the car. He felt as if *he'd* been hit by that articulated lorry which had just rumbled passed them.

The policeman walked back towards them carrying a holdall, which had been in the boot of Jeremy's car.

He opened the door of the police car to speak to them, 'It's over now, for him anyway. Look what we have here, Sir, a bag full of drugs, by the looks of it, he's for the high jump, he'll be old and grey when he surfaces from jail. Attempted murder and drug dealing, he's even got Interpol after him, so we have just been informed, who knows what else he's been up to. He's going down, I'll bet my pension on it. While we wait, can we take a statement from you both, do you feel up to it?'

Tom saw the other policeman handcuff and drag the whimpering bloody mess, which had been the "Amazing" Jeremy; none too gently to the embankment clear of the road.

The next day, Tom was sitting with Jennifer on the settee in his home, resting his bandaged leg on the footstool, and reading the morning paper. His name was plastered all over the newspaper. *"Internationally Renowned Artist Apprehends Wanted Drug Dealer."*

'It's only a few months since I was sat on a seat by the sea, not a care in the world, expecting life to pass me quietly by as I drifted off into total obscurity. Then I took a lady for a drink, and an H-bomb exploded in my life, and I'm still being hit by the fallout.'

'Oh, sounds like some regrets,' said Jennifer, her brows furrowed.

'Not a chance, I wouldn't change a thing... *no*, that's not true,' he said looking sadly at her.

'Don't say any more Tom, please,' she said lifting her legs onto the settee and silently cuddling into him. After a while of simply holding him, she said, 'Put your hand there, that's our little girl, can you feel her moving?'

'I feel it.'

'*Her*, Tom.'

'Yes, *her*, are you *so* sure we are having a girl?'

'Yes, it's a girl.'

They both had to attend the preliminary hearing at the Magistrates court. Jeremy was committed to trial at the Crown Court and denied bail so he would spend his time on remand until his trial. On the way out of the court, Jeremy's mother and father pushed passed Tom without a glance or a word.

How the mighty are fallen, Tom thought. 'Do you know Jen, I hoped that they might have said sorry, at the very least, if not to us, to your mum.'

'Finnley, Jeremy's father, has been struck off and banned from practising law, he was suspected of being involved with Jeremy, and bringing his profession into disrepute, the police couldn't prove anything, he had covered his tracks too well.'

'I have never heard this.'

'Mummy told me, she has a large circle of friends, some of whom were also robbed by the amazing Jeremy, she gets to hear everything. Here is something else I'll bet you didn't know, there is the talk of you been given a knighthood.'

'Give over, now you're winding me up.'

'Am I?' Jennifer said smiling.

'Do you know when I was in the hospital, having lost that blood, the hospital Chaplain came to visit me one morning, out of visiting hours. He didn't come especially to see me, as far as I know; it was only part of his grounds. Actually, it was when I was dressing to make my escape. I was in a rush to get back to Manor Park before you came to see me and give me a load of grief.'

'You were very foolish doing that, Tom, you were risking your life.'

'Anyway, I was compelled out of courtesy to sit and talk to him, what a nice guy he was, he prayed for me and read from his bible. The bit that stuck out to me was, "What does it benefit a man if he gains the whole world and loses his life". *You,* are my life, Jen.' Tom took her in his arms and held her.

Tom and Jennifer went to see the plans for the cottages a week late.

'I love that ceiling to floor window looking across the bay, the view will be incredible,' Jennifer commented as they studied the plans. They wanted some minor changes to the drawings, but overall they were both delighted with the architect's interpretation of their ideas.

The builders were employed, and the work was started. They had given the job to a local builder, which fell perfectly in line with Tom and Jennifer's wish to be part of the community. Unfortunately, they were not able to get up to see the work because Jennifer was in too much pain with her back.

It was common to have back pain in the later stages of pregnancy, Jennifer's Gynaecologist had told them. Doctor Hart, however, had said little when they saw her. Tom tried to think positively. He purchased a wheelchair for the days she struggled, and he would push her around the park. She hated being trapped indoors.

'I'm doing this for my sanity, woman,' he told her as he pushed her in the chair. Jennifer grumbled that she felt ridiculous being pushed around like an old woman. 'You are like a bear with a sore head when you think you can't get out.'

Even though Tom tried to make light of it, he knew as *much as* Jennifer wanted to be outside, that even the motion of the wheelchair was too much for her. He could see her gasping at every jolt, no matter how careful he tried to be. They had only gone a short distance before she had more than she could cope with.

'I'm *sorry* Tom, would you take me back now please, I'm tired.' Tom was trying to brush off these pains by joking, to mask his real anxiety. He was thankful for Carolyn to talk to, she was a saint.'

'We need each other Tom, friends, remember,' Carolyn would remind him.

Chapter Twenty-Six

Morning sickness had been a constant problem for Jennifer, in addition to the pain in her hips and back. To add to her woes, she now suspected she was coming down with a cold and wasn't feeling well at all, coughing and spluttering at any exertion.

'How are you feeling this morning, Jen?' Tom asked when she returned from the bathroom.

'*I'm fine*,' she answered abruptly.

'Oh, I only asked!' Tom lent across the bed to her and noticed that she was still wearing her dressing gown.

'Are you cold? Here, slip it off and cuddle into me.' He reached to help her take off her dressing gown and felt her resisting his help. He abruptly lay back on his pillow staring at the ceiling. After a few moments of silence, Tom asked, 'So, how long has that lump been there?' Jennifer didn't respond, 'Come on Jen, it's no good pretending.'

'I have only just noticed it this morning. Tom, I'm frightened, what about our baby?' And she began to cry. She turned to him, and he held her.

'Shush, I'm sure it will work out. I'll ring doctor Hart first thing.'

In the past, Tom had vehemently opposed private health care and had thought several times what a hypocrite he was. Now it was *his* loved ones needing attention, he had scrapped all of his noble principles. Doctor Hart's secretary answered the phone and asked Tom to wait one moment until she'd spoken to the doctor.

Doctor Hart answered, 'Hello, is that Mr Jackson?'

'Yes.'

'I understand you wish to see me.'

'Yes, Jennifer has a lump on her chest at the left-hand side, not big perhaps an inch in diameter, we have just noticed it.'

'Mmm, I'm busy today, can you come to my office at, 5:30pm, I'll see you then? Sorry I can't see you any sooner.'

'That's wonderful, thank you, we'll be there.'

They tried to keep busy all that day, to avoid thinking. Jennifer's mother called and detected all was not well, but they brushed off her concern, not wanting to worry her unnecessarily.

Tom was thankful that he had taken the time to learn to drive. Jennifer was not in any fit state to be at the wheel of a car, and he was only marginally better.

They were shown straight into the doctor's office, and she stood to welcome them. 'It's so kind of you to see us at such short notice, Doctor Hart.'

'I told you, I understand what you are going through and I do care. Now let me have a look at this lump.' Jennifer removed her coat and loosened her blouse. 'Hmm, I am afraid it is as you suspected.' Tom hugged Jennifer, kissing her head.

'She is coming down with a cold, Doctor, which is not helping things.'

'Tom, I will be honest with you, I don't think Jennifer has a cold.'

'You can't know that,' the doctor only frowned. Tom had never known any feeling like this. There was no natural reaction because this was not natural, his brain had no previous experience to draw on. He couldn't think. He released Jennifer, his hands were trembling; he clung to the arms of his chair.

After a quiet moment, Jennifer raised her head and in a voice filled with panic, asked, 'What about my baby?'

The doctor gazed down at her pen, which she rolled back and forth between her fingers; clearly, this was difficult for her too. Then she looked at Jennifer. 'I won't pretend this is straightforward, we should give you treatment as soon as possible, but, such treatment will undoubtedly endanger your baby. These are difficult decisions for you to make. Whatever you decide I will do all I can, you can be assured of that.'

'I don't have to think about it, I won't have any treatment which might risk my baby's health, *never*.'

'Wait a moment Jen! We should talk about this.'

'No Tom, there is nothing to talk about, I am most likely going to die anyway, I will do all I can for my baby, that will be my gift to you.' Tom was unable to speak; his emotions were in utter turmoil, he couldn't move, when his trembling ceased, he merely stared straight-ahead, he felt utterly paralysed. Jennifer sat with her eyes cast down.

After several minutes, Tom blinked, shook his head slightly, and reached over to put his arm around Jennifer.

'Listen, I'm going to leave you now,' said the doctor, 'I suggest that you sit here quietly until you feel able to go. I will ask the nurse at the desk, just outside my office, to see you are not disturbed. My advice to you both is, go home, be with each other, ring me in the morning and we will take it from there. Tom wiped his face with his hand, thanked the doctor, and she left, squeezing Tom's shoulder as she passed him.

That was how they remained for some time, eventually, Tom said, 'I love you, Jen, we face everything together, that's the deal, remember? If you feel up to it, let's go and grab a cup of coffee somewhere before we head off home.' Tom hadn't a clue where he was drawing this strength from, he sounded so sensible and rational, but he knew he was an utter wreck. Jennifer only nodded her head. Tom stood and raised Jennifer into his arms.

They didn't go for coffee, Jennifer said she only wanted to go home, so they strolled back to the car.

As they travelled home, Tom said, 'We will have to go and tell your mum, she has the right to know. Perhaps we could walk up to see her later this evening, or I will go on my own if you don't feel up to it?'

'No, it's all right I will come with you. I'll be all right once we are home and I have had a cup of tea. It's just that I have been feeling so well, up until recently. We've had a wonderful time, haven't we, Tom?' She looked at him begging him to say he had no regrets. Tom managed to smile; he was filled with such love for her.

'Yes we have, darling, it's been the best.'

'This news is a bit of a blow, that's all. We always knew this was going to happen. I'll have to settle this in my mind and move on, sorry to be such a frightful bore, Tom.'

Chapter Twenty-Seven

Jennifer's health deteriorated rapidly over the subsequent weeks. She was struggling to breathe and became breathless with the least amount of effort. Walking was a problem too, she was in dreadful pain, Tom could only surmise how much pain, she rarely, if ever, complained. If she saw him looking at her, she would always try to smile, and he would dutifully attempt to return her smile, but nobody was kidding anybody. It was all some macabre game being played out.

She had been given a walking frame by the hospital, but she would rather struggle than use it, much to Tom's annoyance.

'Your pride may well come "Literally" before a fall, you annoying woman,' Tom was driven by frustration to say. Jennifer responded by sticking out her tongue at him. 'Ahhh, I give up,' he said playfully punching her on the nose.

Reluctantly, Jennifer had succumbed to using a walking stick, but only if it was not mentioned.

Tom was sure everything was made worse because she had little appetite and was growing weaker by the day.

He *never* imagined how hard this would be. He always knew it would be hell, but he *never* thought that it would be anything like this. Helplessly, watching the one you loved dying by inches and that was all he could do, listen. Her braveness only served to intensify and highlight his weakness. If there was Hell on earth this was it, there could be no doubt now, Jennifer was going to die, the only uncertainty was their baby, the longer Jennifer could carry it, the greater chance of survival it had.

This was Jennifer's choice, she had chosen to forgo treatment, to give her life for their baby, and Tom resolved to respect that that was her decision. He knew how important it was, in a future out of her control to be able to make a positive choice, no matter how painful it was for him.

She had literally cancelled any hope of her survival. If it had been up to him, he would have grasped at any straw, which was offered. He knew that, but that was from his point of view. Perhaps, I would have seen things differently if I had been in Jennifer's shoes, he thought. Tom's mind was so tired, he couldn't think straight, what he thought changed from minute to minute. All he knew for sure was that the thought of being without Jennifer crippled him.

"This is hell", was his constant silent cry. Jennifer was asleep, a rare relief from her torment. Tom went into the kitchen to make himself a cup of tea and leant against the sink. He was so tired; he stood for some time, trying to think *why* he'd come into the kitchen. His brain was mush; he shook his head, remembering, and wearily made himself some tea. He didn't know why he was bothering he didn't even want a drink.

He put some sugar in the cup stirred the tea, took a sip, and wandered out into the garden to the rustic garden bench, which looked back towards the house. The garden wasn't big, but it was private and well stocked with flowers, Phil from the big house looked after it for them. Tom was no gardener, and he didn't have any time to learn, that brief moment had past. Jennifer would tell him all the names of the flowers while they sat on the bench, she even knew their botanical names, but he couldn't remember them. That was another place another time.

It was autumn now, and the garden was passed its best, but there was some late flowering honeysuckle near the bench where he sat, he remembered that. The fragrance washed over him, its beauty was almost a denial of the ugliness with which he was faced.

It all just goes on, come what may, he thought. He was compelled to give a sad smile as he watched the swallows swooping and soaring as they chased the small insects.

He leant forward on his knees, mindlessly gazing at the steaming cup in his hands. He shook his head despairingly, sighed and glanced up, his eye caught sight of a blackbird scampering across the lawn. Periodically it would stop and turn its head as if listening, and then it would stab his beak into the ground and tug at a worm. Tom shook his head at the moment's distraction, sighed again, and gazed once more at his cup, rolling it back and forth in the palms of his hands.

'I can't cope with this, if there is a God out there listening, I just want you to know, Jen needs my support, I need to be strong for her, but I can hardly drag myself around, let alone support her. She is the one suffering and has a right to expect me to be strong, but I'm not, I am weak, it's too much all this.' All he could hear were the words of the preacher, from his first visit to church going around and around in his head, "Do you know that I love you?"

'That's utter rubbish. If you loved me, *you*, who can do anything, you would make this mess right. Jennifer has done nothing wrong. If you are punishing her for something, then there is no hope for anyone. She is the kindest, most loving person I have ever known, it's simply not fair.' Again the words came, "Do you know that I love you?"

'Okay, you love me, big deal; I can't see it, if you loved me, you would be suffering my torments too and do something about it. I would give my life for the ones I loved, and a voice in his head said, "I did".' At that moment a warmth and peace swept over Tom, he couldn't understand it, in fact, he was afraid, all he said was, 'God – loves – me,' and began to cry. For the first time since all this started, he felt that he really would not be alone, and would be able to cope. Not laughing and dancing, but he knew he would cope. He was startled unexpectedly, as a hand touched his shoulder. It was Jennifer.

'Ah! Jen, you were asleep, you should have waited for me, what if you fell! I came out to enjoy the sunshine. For a moment I was remembering sitting on a bench on another sunny day...' His voice trailed off, he couldn't finish the sentence.

'Don't be cross, Tom? I wondered where you were, that's all.' Jennifer came around and sat beside him, and he hugged her.

'Dear, dear, Jennifer, where is your walking stick, I can't bear to see you struggling. I know the constant pain you are in, why didn't you call me?'

'Don't worry Tom, I'm all right, you never stop running after me, I'm wearing you out. It upsets me to see how tired you are sometimes, don't deny it.'

'Jen, honestly, I want to do this, anyway I don't have a choice, I can't help it. You would do the same for me. Look, I don't want to talk like this. Tell you what, let's go inside and make mad passionate love.'

'What! With this great bump in front of me,' she laughed, 'how much bigger can I get before I burst?' She ran her fingers through his hair and then rested her head on his shoulder. 'Tom I love you. I wish it could have been different, the time has been so short.'

'Hey, I have been given something very extraordinary. I have known a love that most people only dream of, and I am okay, just, but I am okay.' He tipped out the dregs of tea onto the soil and stood up. He carefully helped her up and held her, supporting her as they returned to the house. He knew the cancer was in her bones now and she was in constant agony, though she attempted to hide it from him. He didn't care what anyone said; he knew it was possible for a human being to feel another's pain, for he could feel Jennifer's. Every time she winced, he was touched with a red-hot iron.

Once inside Tom gently removed her dressing gown, then she sat on the side of the bed, he lifted her legs up and slid her slowly around supporting her back as she lay down. He saw her holding her lip between her teeth to prevent her crying out, but he said nothing. She let out a long breath as she settled back into the pillows, and attempted a smile. Tom was choking, he couldn't speak, she is one hundred fold stronger than I am, he thought and he too tried to smile, leaning down and resting his lips to her cheek. He knew this little exercise had worn her out. She wasn't even able to lift her arm to hold him.

'Try to get some sleep, Jen, I'll sit in this armchair, so you relax, if you need anything I'll be right here.'

'Will you lie beside me Tom and hold my hand?'

'Sure I will if that's what you want,' he didn't want to get on the bed next to her because he knew the pain it would cause as his weight disturbed the bed. He tried to be as careful as he could, but she couldn't prevent a groan when the mattress dipped as he lay down, causing her to be twisted slightly, 'Sorry Jen.'

'It will be all right Tom, it's worth it,' she panted, in a soft barely audible voice.

Chapter Twenty-Eight

Tom had fallen asleep, he was suddenly awoken by Jennifer's groaning. She cried out. He had been in such a deep sleep that at first, he didn't know where he was. Jennifer's distress caused him to rouse himself quickly.

'What is it, Jen?'

'It's the baby, Tom, I think it's coming, AHHH! Tom, help me, it's agony.'

'But it's not due for another six weeks. Wait a minute, wait a minute, let me think. Right, I'll ring the emergency number 999, for an ambulance.' Fortunately, they had a telephone by the bedside. Tom explained the problem and the girl who answered said they would be with them in a few minutes. 'Thank God we only live ten minutes from the hospital.'

Jennifer was screaming in agony, Tom knew cancer in her body was magnifying every spasm. He was beside himself; he couldn't think what to do to ease her suffering, her head was covered in beads of sweat. Tom rang Doctor Hart too; she had told them to ring if the baby came early, in fact, if there was an emergency. She had been so kind. Tom suspected that because of her own loss to this illness, she had gone beyond anything that was demanded of her professionally. Tom heard the bell of the ambulance and a screech of brakes, there was a knock on the door. It was Doctor Hart; Tom was stunned for a second, 'Doctor Hart, what, what?'

'I was on my way home when you rang, so I came straight here, where is she?'

'Through there.' Not that there could be much doubt, Jennifer was screaming the place down. The doctor pushed past him and made towards Jennifer's cries. Tom was so confused that he almost closed the door on the two ambulance men. They pushed past him, carrying a stretcher. He followed them all into the bedroom.

'I have given her an injection to ease the pain,' Doctor Hart said, then she turned to the ambulance men, 'make sure she is strapped to that stretcher; treat her as a spinal injury. Tom, I will go now and meet you back at the hospital, the injection will take hold in a moment, and then she will be more comfortable. It won't take long to get her to the hospital, I will have everything organised for her when you get there.'

'I don't know what to say, I can't tell you how much I appreciate this,' but she wasn't listening, she dashed out before he had finished thanking her. Jennifer had actually calmed as the two men lifted her into the ambulance.

Doctor Hart was waiting for them when they arrived at the hospital as she had promised. Doctor Hart told them to take Jennifer straight down to the theatre near the maternity ward. Jennifer was calm now. Tom held her hand as they pushed her on a trolley and Doctor Hart walked with them.

Tom could see the word "Theatre" ahead of them. Doctor Hart touched his arm saying, 'Listen, Tom, you will have to wait in here,' pointing to a small waiting room with chairs.

'Jennifer won't know you're not there, she is sedated.'

'But I must be with her, you see, I promised.'

'I'm sorry Tom, she is going into theatre, she will have to have a caesarean section, do you remember? We would only be a hindrance, and we don't want that, do we?'

'No, no of course not.'

'It is a simple procedure, remember, we discussed it. Jennifer would never be able to give birth normally she is too weak. They will give her anaesthetic; she won't be in any more pain. She is a courageous lady, I'm sure you are very proud of her; she is an example to us all. You sit there I'll organise a cup of tea and come back to you.' The doctor took his arm and steered him to a chair.

Doctor Hart returned before he had time to think, with two cups on a tray and passed him one, set the tray on a table and sat with him.

'Jennifer won't be in any pain Tom so you can relax, it will take about an hour,' she looked at her watch and glanced up to a clock on the wall. Doctor Hart tried to engage Tom in conversation, to distract him, asking if they had thought of any names. Did he want a boy or a girl? She told him the actual delivery would only take about ten minutes.

'Once your baby is delivered, Jennifer will be taken into a room, to give her time to recover from the anaesthetic, and then you will be able to sit with her. As soon as she comes around, we will bring her baby to her.' Tom nodded to the doctor, but his anxiety for Jennifer was such that none of the information was making much sense. The time seemed to pass inordinately quickly. It felt as if they had only just sat down when a nurse came in and told Tom that the delivery went well, and he was now the father of a beautiful little girl who weighed 5lb 3oz. He tried to speak but he couldn't. It was almost as if he was somewhere else, merely an observer.

'Go with the nurse Tom, she will show you where Jennifer is, Tom,' Doctor Hart repeated, she could see how he was struggling.

'Oh, yes, right, with the nurse.'

'I will give you a few moments then I will come in. I want to take a look at Jennifer.'

The nurse took Tom's arm and led him to Jennifer's room. He was relieved to see her she looked so peaceful, after the long weeks of torture. He reached for a chair, set it by the bed, and flopped down, taking her hand tenderly in his. He kissed it and pressed it against his cheek. 'I love you, Jen, can you hear me? Those words will be on my lips for the rest of my life. I love you, and you will never know how much.'

Doctor Hart entered, and he made to stand. 'It's all right Tom, I'll go around the other side, you just sit still I won't be a moment,' and she proceeded to listen to Jennifer's chest with her stethoscope and felt her pulse.

'How is she, Doctor?' The doctor pulled out a chair from under a table and sat down too, she was quiet for some moments, clearly trying to find the right words.

'Tom, I told you that I would always tell you the truth, to the best of my ability,' she paused, 'Jennifer is very weak, she has literally given her life for your daughter.'

Tom lowered his head, trying desperately to control himself but he just couldn't. His body shook, and tears spilt from his eyes, he didn't want to hear this. He took out his handkerchief, wiped his eyes, and blew his nose.

'It's all right Doctor, you don't need to say anything.'

'I'm so very sorry Tom.'

'Thank you, Doctor, for all the time and kindness you have given Jennifer and me, you could not have done more.'

'Tom, we doctors are not machines. I, for one care about my patients, too much probably. I have never been very good at separating myself from my work. It has been a privilege to have this time with you and Jennifer... Tom, I must say this... I don't think Jennifer will pull around her pulse is very weak. You may only have a few moments, perhaps she will last out the rest of the day, I hope so, so she is able to see your baby.'

Tom was a wreck he was falling apart, he blurted out, 'You see, I love her Doctor, I can't be without her it's not... it's not.' The Doctor touched his arm.

'I know, Tom, I know. I remember only too vividly. I came to realise that how I felt, meant that what my husband and I had, was very precious, a treasure, and as the time went on that gave me a great deal of comfort. To love with all your heart is a great gift.'

Tears were running down the doctor's face now, and she touched *her* eyes with her handkerchief. 'Look, Tom, Jennifer is waking, I'll go and send the nurse in with your baby girl, you gave me a long list of names when Jennifer was in theatre, have you decided what to call her?'

'Yes, err, yes, Jennifer, Margaret.'

'How beautiful, just one moment,' and the doctor left quietly closing the door. The sight of Jennifer's flickering eyes was enough to calm Tom. He wiped his face once more, blew his nose again, and then took her hand.

'Hello, Mother.' He smiled, and she returned his smile. 'How do you feel?'

'Thirsty,' she croaked, 'how's our baby, Tom?' She looked anxiously at him.

'Need you ask? It's a girl, and she is perfect, they are bringing her here, as we speak.' There were a glass and a jug of water on the cupboard by the bedside. He poured her some. Fortunately, there was a straw in the glass, he touched it to her lips, and she took a sip.

'Thank you, Tom, that's nectar.' As he set the glass back on the cupboard, the nurse entered with their baby and laid her next to her mother.

'I want her to be called after you, Jennifer Margaret.'

'I always said the choice was yours, thank you, Tom,' she whispered. 'Tom, she is beautiful...' and a tear ran from Jennifer's eye onto the babies head as she gently pressed her lips to her babies cheek. Tom touched the tear tenderly with his finger and pressed it to his lips.

'She is the image of her beautiful mother.' Tom's voice shook; he managed to control himself, *just*.

Jennifer smiled again at him. 'You have always spoiled me Tom; I knew it would be a girl. I love you; you will never know how happy you have made me. Don't be sad, it has been perfect, hasn't it? And look what we have to show for our love.'

'Yes...' Tom held his lip between his teeth.

'Look, Tom,' she turned her eyes to the window and smiled, 'our swallows, they've come to see our new baby.'

Tom raised his head and glanced through the window. The swallows were sitting on the telephone wires just outside the room.

'So they have.' Suddenly, there was a flutter of wings, and they left, his eyes returned to her face... her eyes had closed... he knew she was at peace now.

Chapter Twenty-Nine

Tom was sitting on his bench looking along the beach as he had countless times before.

He sat there so often, locals called it, "Tom's Bench". He never said, but when he sat on the bench gazing into the distance towards the castle, it was always his hope that he might see a beautiful young woman in a white dress, coming towards him, carrying a sun-hat in her hand. Just a glimpse for a second, he would give anything for only one second.

Sometimes, he thought he had seen her, and for that brief moment, he was complete again, his ache eased, and the years fell away.

He glanced down at his gold Rolex watch and stroked the bezel with his thumb, as he always did when he thought of her. It was worn now; the serrated pattern, which had been around the edge, had long since been rubbed smooth.

'Hmm,' he said, breathing out a slow sigh as he remembered that Christmas morning so many years ago.

He wondered if anyone could understand his sadness. It was more than a torment of the mind; the first thing he was conscious of when he awoke was the physical pain, the sickness inside. Before he even had time to consciously think of her it was there. He wondered if this was what people meant when they talked of a broken heart. No, he doubted that she would never break his heart, but he did know that part of him had gone with her when she left, and the wound had never healed. He knew it never would, not while they were separated. Sometimes the pain was so intense he couldn't go about his daily work, he had to sit until some strength returned and he was able to go on. He said little about how he felt, what was the point? The pain now, was part of the joy then, he was sure of that.

The locals were kind to him, they had all taken to *his* Jennifer, he was a local now, almost, and known to all as the "Swallow Painter". As he pondered mindlessly the passage of time, his eye lighted on a fisherman in a blue jersey, carrying a lobster pot. The fisherman shouted to him, 'Coming for a pint of shandy, Tom?'

'Good idea, later maybe, Bill, it's your around don't forget.'

'You poor artists are all the same,' Bill laughed, as he walked on across the rectangle to his house in the corner.

Shandy – that was what we had that first night in the smoke-filled pub, he reflected sadly. He wondered how many times that scene had been played out in his mind over the years? He remembered every moment. Whenever he went in or came out of the pub, he would pause at the point where she had impulsively reached up and kissed him. How she had embarrassed herself. He knew he wouldn't go to the pub tonight. He was too tired, and anyway, he was sitting with a beautiful reporter who wanted to interview him, she smiled at him.

'So then, Sir Thomas Jackson, knighted for services to art, you must be the North East's most famous artist and you have never given an interview for the North East Gazette before, is that correct?'

'Famous, is that what I am? Believe me, it's dry ground at the top of that hill.' Tom smiled, he remembered meeting John Lennon, and he called himself "A fool on a hill". 'Anyway, as far as I can recall, this is the first time I have been asked for an interview.'

'Shameful, well… we will correct that woeful oversight right now. First of all, can I ask what's so extraordinary about this spot, beautiful though it is, there must be more to it than that?'

'This is where my life began. I met my wife, and inspiration, here on this seat; I would have been nothing without her. You are sitting exactly where she sat.'

He lifted his walking stick and pointed along the beach, 'Do you see along there, where those two dogs are playing in the surf?'

'Yes.'

'That's where I saw her for the first time. She was returning from her walk to the castle at Dunstanburgh. She had arrived earlier that afternoon for a holiday, and the first thing she did was to walk to the castle. She came up the steps there,' he pointed again with his stick, 'laughing and telling me I was in her seat.'

'Was it love at first sight?'

'Near enough, but anyone who saw her would have fallen in love with her, who could help it, it was her smile, it brought colour and life to everything it touched. God only knows what she saw in me. However, Jennifer, I have told you about your mum often enough, you could write this article on your own,' she squeezed the old man's hand.

'I never tire of you telling me, Dad, you told me the swallows had just arrived that day, now it's autumn and time for them to go again, the summer's almost over.'

'Yes, the dark nights are cutting in.' He glanced up at the telephone wires and the lines of swallows sitting there, fluttering their wings, eager to be off to places new.

'That moment has stayed with you, everyone calls you the Swallow Painter or Swallow Man.'

'I can't imagine why,' he smiled, 'but I'm worn out now with all your questions, come on let's walk up to the cottages, and you can make me a cup of tea, that will be my payment for this exclusive interview.' She offered her hand and pulled him up. Tom's daughter Jennifer wasn't only the chief reporter for the Gazette; she owned the paper since her grandmother died.

They linked arms and slowly strolled up the hill to the cottages where he and *his* Jennifer had their first meal together.

'No regrets about giving up teaching, dad.'

'Now you are teasing me,' he laughed, 'none whatsoever. I was hopeless. I hated every moment. Did you know Jennifer, that they asked me back years later to give a talk to the whole school?'

'No, how did that go?'

'The biggest laugh was, that the Head was one of the "Little darlings" who made my life a misery. He told me what an inspiration I had been. What a liar, I thought here's a bloke who knows how to say the right thing, no wonder he's made it to be Headmaster.' Jennifer laughed.

'You're ever the cynic, Dad. You never wanted to marry again?'

'No, any woman would have come second place to your mum. I told her she would be the only woman for me, and she was, she was perfect. I have never for one second regretted loving her, and I have never *stopped* loving her. My only regret is that you never got a chance to know her, to see her smile, or hear her laugh, she laughed so easily. She even laughed at my jokes,' he nudged his daughter and she smiled.

'I feel to know her, Dad, you make her alive as you talk, and that portrait you painted is unbelievable, I used to touch it when I was small, I expected her to speak to me.'

'I remember, you used to ask me to take it off the wall so you could touch it. When I carried you through to bed, you would always say, "Kiss Mamma", and you would kiss her. That's all a long time since now.'

'Do you really think of Mother all the time?'

'All the time.'

'You never thought to marry Doctor Hart, she was your closest friend as long as I can remember?'

'Your aunty Lynn, no, we never had that sort of relationship. She was a good friend, the very best, along with your grandmother. Aye... and I loved them, they're both gone now, aye...' he repeated, stopping and staring down at the tip of his walking stick, twisting it back and forth in the dust. 'But I still have you, you've always been the gift your mum promised,' and he squeezed her hand, giving her a weak smile. She could see the tears in his eyes. 'Your grandma and Lynn were always there for me after your mum died. Well, in truth we were there for each other. Our friendship was good for us all, we understood each other's pain. We didn't even have to talk about it, that's very special in a friendship. I believe God once told me I would not be on my own, and Lynn was a blessing, but it could never have been anything more.'

The alterations to the three cottages had been completed many years ago, and they were now one house. Tom was always sorry Jennifer never got to see them finished. He knew he could never have coped with anyone else living next door to him, that's why he had bought all three.

He had painted a nameplate for the three houses, that were now one house, it had a swallow painted in the corner, and the name he had painted on was "Number three", that was their name now. He never told anyone why, but that's where his heart was, at number three. He lived there most of the time it was home to him, he said he felt nearer to her when he was there.

As they neared the cottage, he asked his daughter to stop for a moment, saying he was out of breath. While they stood, he took out his pocketknife, reached into the hedge, and cut out a dog rose. Holding it in his now wrinkled hand, he lifted the flower to his nose and smiled, and they set off again, continuing up to the house.

'Funny thing this one rose flowering, it's late, out of season, perhaps a gift for me. It's very fragile... *aye*... very fragile, you must make the most of things while you can. We take so much for granted and don't see the gift God has given us to hold, it might be merely for a moment, like this rose and then it's gone.'

Jennifer noticed blood running down his hand, 'Dad! You've cut your wrist.'

'It's nothing, Jen,' he said, pausing and glancing down at it. He smiled, he was reminded of a similar scratch all those years ago or was it just yesterday.

'Aye,' he gave a long sigh, 'so I have, it doesn't hurt it'll be fine.' For a brief moment in the evening sunlight, he saw *his* beloved Jennifer as he glanced at his daughter. She was her image, he knew that, but for that brief moment, he could have sworn...

When they reached the whitewashed cottage where he lived, Tom turned, and momentarily looked down the hill to where he had been seated, it was odd, he thought he heard *her* call. He shook his head and turned back to his house.

'Come on love, let's get in.' His daughter leant against the front door with her shoulder and gave it a sharp push to open it, 'I wish you would get this door fixed Dad, it's been difficult to open as long as I can remember.'

'Ha, I like it like that.'

'You sit down Dad, while I make us a cuppa, here give me your hat and coat.' As she leant forward, he kissed her cheek, and she returned the kiss.

'I love you Dad.'

'Aye, I know lass.' He walked over to the fireside and eased himself down into his chair. She stood for a moment and watched him gazing at the rose he'd cut from the hedge, slowly rolling it back and forth between his finger and thumb. He glanced up at *her* portrait that hung on the wall facing him, the two of them by the fire, as always, and he nodded to her likeness.

Jennifer smiled, and went over to him and hugged him once more, kissing the top of his head, placing her hands on his shoulders. He laid his hand on hers, patting it affectionately and smiled up at her. With a slight squeeze of her fingers, she let go of his shoulders, slowly running her fingertips across his back, as she went into the kitchen to make the tea.

It was only five minutes before she returned with the two steaming mugs on a tray, she abruptly stopped... her dad was smiling, his chin resting on his chest, she glanced at his hand, it was empty, the rose lay on the floor by his side... she knew as he had always told her,

"Swallows Leave In Autumn".

THE END

Above all Powers

Above all powers,
Above all kings,
Above all nature,
And all created things,
Above all wisdom,
And all the ways of man,
You were here,
Before the world began.

Above all kingdoms,
Above all thrones,
Above all wonders,
The world has ever known,
Above all wealth,
And treasures of the earth,
There's no way to measure,
What You're worth.

Crucified,
Laid behind a stone,
You lived to die,
Rejected and alone,
Like a rose,
Trampled on the ground,
You took the fall,
And thought of *me*.
Above all

Michael W. Smith

Other books by this author:

Restoration (Book 1)

This is a saga is spread over two novels, telling of impossible love, its path travelled, and the tension between relationships, honour, pride, privilege, resentment, hate, and forgiveness.

Acceptance (Book 2)

The series plot a family's journey through the period of history from 1900 to 1946 the fears, sadness, and uncertainties of two world wars with their lottery of life and death, the only constant is love and the product of love, hope.
Set in the North East of England.

The Man Who Lived In A Book

A murder mystery set in the Marshall Islands. You may well solve the murder but miss the mystery.

Detective Inspector Tyyamii has a great future, how would you like to be his assistant in the Marshall Islands?

Dream World

William the Conqueror could never have imagined the impact that gruesome October day on Senlac ridge would have.
This story puts flesh on the names and breath in the lungs of the people, etched into every English person's psyche from school days.

Jarl Magnus Matthewson, from Northumbria, is faced with the moral choices conflicting with loyalty, honour, and friendship, and his concern for those who place their simple trust in him.
"Live history with him."

A Warrior's Inheritance

Sequel to "Dream World"; Magnus' grandchildren are subjected to violent mysteries, and they are in danger of losing all there grandfather left in their care.

The Colour of Envy

This story is set in the reign of Henry II arguably one of England's greatest kings. Unfortunately, his reign is forever overshadowed by the murder of Thomas Becket.

On hearing of the fortunes to be made at the tournais in France, a young knight

Richard Maillorie rides away from his impoverished home hoping to restore the family's wealth. He is handsome, talented, successful, and is invited to become part of the acclaimed William Marshal's elite band of warriors. They soon become firm friends both having the highest ideals of honour and self-sacrifice.

When Richard returns to England, he is preceded by his fame and asked to attend King Henry's court.

Richard falls in love, but his relationships are complicated by the very ideals that set him above his peers.

Printed in Great Britain
by Amazon